B A D

BAD

JEAN FERRIS

FARRAR STRAUS GIROUX   NEW YORK

Copyright © 1998 by Jean Ferris
All rights reserved
Distributed in Canada by Douglas & McIntyre Ltd.
Printed in the United States of America
Designed by Filomena Tuosto
First edition, 1998

Library of Congress Cataloging-in-Publication Data
Ferris, Jean, date.
    Bad / Jean Ferris. — 1st ed.
        p.   cm.
    Summary: In an attempt to please her friends, sixteen-year-old Dallas goes along with their plan
to rob a convenience store and when her father refuses to allow her to come home, she is sen-
tenced to six months in the Girls' Rehabilitation Center.
    ISBN 0-374-30479-3
    [1. Juvenile delinquency—Fiction.]   I. Title.
PZ7.F4174Bad   1998
[Fic]—dc21   97-44197

Excerpt from *The Member of the Wedding* reprinted by permission of Houghton Mifflin Co. Copyright © 1946 by Carson McCullers, renewed © 1974 by Florida V. Lasky. All rights reserved

"In Me" and "[Oh Yes, My Dear, Oh Yes]" reprinted with the permission of Simon & Schuster from
Mirror of the Heart: Poems of Sara Teasdale, edited and introduced by William Drake. Copyright ©
1984 by the Morgan Guaranty Trust Company of New York. From the Collection of American Literature, the Beinecke Rare Book and Manuscript Library, Yale University

"Dreams" reprinted by permission of Alfred A. Knopf, Inc., from *Collected Poems* by Langston
Hughes. Copyright © 1994 by the Estate of Langston Hughes

SKIDMORE COLLEGE LIBRARY

To the memory of Jane O'Neil
To live, to love, to learn, to leave a legacy

This book grew from a series of interviews I did in the summer of 1993 with girls at the Girls' Rehabilitation Facility, a division of the Juvenile Court, in San Diego. The girls had initially invited me to talk about one of my books *(Across the Grain)*, which had been nominated for the California Young Readers' Medal, and then invited me back to see if I could find a book in their experiences. They were extraordinarily generous in talking to me. They told me anything I wanted to know—and occasionally more than I wanted to know—about their gang lives, their criminal lives, their sex lives, and their drug lives. Their stories were hair-raising and heartbreaking and sometimes even hilarious. What they were reluctant to talk about were their family lives: the places where the greatest hurts lay. I became quite fond of these girls. Their street smarts, survival instincts, and premature adulthood have made them tough survivors as well as blighted children. I wish peaceful, happy, abundant futures for them all, even as I know (and so do they) the odds of that.

This book is for them, those fierce and wounded girls.

With many thanks to Mary Glover of the San Diego County Department of Education, who started this all; to Arlene Smith, Public Affairs Coordinator for Probation, and Judge William Pate, then Presiding Judge of Juvenile Court, for their help with greasing the bureaucratic wheels; to Jane O'Neil, teacher and mother hen at GRF for her compassion and humor; to Jeff Reilly in the Office of the Public Defender for his help with how the system works—any license I've taken is my own and not due to any fault of his; to Phyllis Nemeth, whose Project Night Light at the California Youth Authority in Norwalk inspired the bedtime stories used in this book; to my friends Superior Court Judge Thomas Ashworth and attorney Kathryn Ashworth for guidance; to Kerry Ferris for many articles, clippings, and stories; and to my favorite attorney in the world, Al Ferris, for being my first reader.

J.F.

B A D

ONE

I knew what my father was going to say before he said it.

"You're turning out just like your mother."

Good, I thought. At least she knew how to have fun. She hadn't sat at home moping and thinking up new rules to make things hard for everybody else the way he did.

"You tell me that all the time," I said, my hands on my hips, my heart rate in overdrive. "Like it's a crime. What if I think it's a good thing?"

"Then you're seriously wrong," he said, standing in front of the door, blocking my exit. "And seriously misguided. Don't forget she was drunk when she cracked herself up in the car. At three in the afternoon. With the guy from next door, who should have been at work so he could support his wife and kids. You can't tell me that's a good thing."

I was only four when she died. All I could remember of her is how she smelled and the jingle of her silver bracelets and the way things felt more exciting when she was around. Even then I think I understood that she knew what a good time was all about, while my father wouldn't know one if it came bow-tied and special delivery. Okay, so maybe she overdid it, but she managed to get in a lot of living before she ran out of time.

I wondered if she knew how much trouble she'd left behind.

"You're not leaving here tonight," my father said. "I know you're going to meet that boy. He's bad news and you know it. I've been telling you that for the last six months, from the day you met him. If you leave here, you're admitting what you want is to get into trouble."

He was right. Ray *was* bad news—but that was part of his appeal. And I probably would get into trouble. But when I was with Ray, things happened. There was excitement and action, filling me, proving I was there. At home, at school—when I managed to get there—everything seemed to be in slow motion and muted colors. I felt hollow and barely visible.

Ray called it *skating* when we did the crazy things—grabbing an old lady's purse when she cut through the park in the late afternoon. Hot-wiring a fancy car for a joyride after midnight. Boosting stuff from stores. Ray liked to take cigarettes. Me, I was so good, I told him I could get away with the sales clerk's pantyhose. I had a drawer full of clothes and jewelry I'd taken but wouldn't wear. It was the skating, not the stuff, that I liked.

The one skaty thing I really didn't like was the way Ray sometimes insisted on sex in public places: quick, up against a wall, in an alley in the daytime, or slow, on a golf course at night, even when it was cold out. But I knew he'd be in a good mood after, happy with me, and that made it worth it.

"You're not Ray's favorite person, either," I said to my father. "He says your rule book must be a foot thick."

"Just like his skull. Why don't you understand that what I'm trying to do is protect you? I know what a mess somebody like your mother leaves behind her, and I don't want your life to be as messy as Dixie Lee's."

Dixie Lee. I loved my mother's name. It sounded spirited

and lively. I knew it must have been her idea to name me Dallas. Dear old Dad would never have thought of something like that.

"Well, you picked her," I said. "Don't blame me."

"And I'm paying for it," he said, almost inaudibly. "I don't care if you are only sixteen; if you leave this house tonight, I'll take no responsibility for what happens to you next."

"Great," I said, pushing my way around him to the door.

"That'll be a relief to us both." I ignored the sick lurch my stomach always took when he said he'd had enough of me, even if I didn't think he meant it. I'd go meet Ray. We'd do some skating. I'd sleep at Pam's, the way I'd done plenty of other times, until he calmed down. I'd be okay.

Ray was at the café where we usually met. Pam, my best friend for the past two years, and Sonny, her boyfriend and Ray's best friend, were with him, drinking coffee and working on a big plate of fries. Pam and Sonny had fixed me up with Ray, and since then I'd finally had a feeling of belonging somewhere, of having my own group. I didn't ever want to be without them.

"Hey, babe," Ray said to me, snaking his arm around my waist and pulling me into the booth. "We figured you were duking it out with your old man." He dragged me up against him. He was warm and solid and for that moment I felt safe. "You win?"

"I'm here, aren't I?" I said. "What's happening?"

"As far as Pam's folks are concerned," Sonny said, his arm around Pam's shoulders, "she's baby-sitting. Too bad your old man's not as easy to fool as they are."

"I'm a much better liar than Dallas is," Pam said.

She looked like a second-grader, with her cute short haircut and her little white blouse, so it was no big job to see why she could fool her parents whenever she wanted to. But she liked skating as much as I did, though for different reasons. She got off on how easy it was to fool people, to rip them off, to get them to believe her lies. It made her feel superior.

It made me feel alive.

"We were thinking we might try something different tonight," Ray said. "Something a little . . . skatier."

"Like what?" I still felt breathless, partly from rushing to get there, partly from the showdown with my father.

"Look," Pam said. She handed her purse across the table. "Look inside."

I opened it. Next to the wallet, keys, and other junk was a small, shiny silver pistol. I looked up at her, startled. "Where'd you get that?" I handed her back the purse as if it contained a live snake.

"It's my dad's. He reported it stolen a couple of months ago, but I'm the one that stole it. I figured it might come in handy sometime. You never know."

"Looks like tonight's the night," Sonny said.

"Why?" I asked. "What's happening tonight?"

"We're going to get some money," Ray said. "You know how you ladies have been wanting to go to Typhoon, but we can't get in because they're so tight about IDs? Well, we need to buy us some fake IDs. And some hot clothes to go with them. We'll be going to Typhoon in style."

"Who's going to give us this money?" I asked.

"Who has the most, this time of night?" Sonny asked.

"Who?" I said. This was the skatiest thing I'd ever been in on. The gun scared me in a way that made my stomach hurt. "Liquor stores?"

"They also have security cameras," Ray said. "Not to mention guns of their own." He waved his hand dismissively. "So they're out. We're after a Jiffy-Spot. They have money and no guns."

"Are you sure?" I asked.

"You ever notice who works in those places? Kids, old folks, foreigners. People without our smarts."

"They still have security cameras," I said.

"Hey, what are you? Chicken?" Ray asked, drawing away from me. "What's with all the objections?"

"I'm not objecting," I insisted. I wanted him next to me again. "I'm just trying to use some of those smarts I'm supposed to have."

Ray laughed and put his arm back around me. "Okay, then. There's a way around security cameras and we've already done it."

"Done what?" I asked.

"First you pick the place," Sonny said. "Then you create a disturbance."

"Which Sonny and I did last night," Ray added. "We knocked over a whole big Super Bowl display. Beer, chips, dips, little footballs. Made a real mess."

"And while Ray and the clerk worked on cleaning it up," Sonny went on, "I got up on the counter and smeared Vaseline on the camera lens. By the time the clerk was back to his post, it was all over and he never knew it happened."

"Vaseline?" I asked.

"Yeah. Blurs the image, but the camera doesn't look tampered with. Pretty slick, huh?"

Pam grinned. "Yeah. Very. Where is this place?"

"Not in our neighborhood, that's for sure," Sonny said. "We don't want to run into somebody who might know us."

I barely listened while they talked. I knew I'd go along with them, whatever they planned. I always did. With them the hollowness inside me was filled enough, even if it came back when I was by myself.

"Well, let's get going," Ray said, giving me a push. "Adventure is waiting."

A fine, cold drizzle had started. I shivered and got into Ray's car. Pam and Sonny were in the back seat.

We stopped in the parking lot of a Jiffy-Spot across town. There were two other cars in the lot, and while we sat there, a man came out of the store, got in one of them, and drove away.

"I'll go in and see what it looks like," Sonny said.

After a few minutes, he came out of the Jiffy-Spot and got back in the car. "Damn, it's getting cold." He rubbed his arms. "Nobody in there except the clerk. That must be his car."

Ray put his hand on my thigh. "We've decided you get to hold the gun."

I started, and Ray gripped my leg harder.

"Me? Why me?"

"You seem sunk tonight, babe. Being behind a weapon'll wake you up. Think of it as vitamins." He laughed. "Vitamins," he said again. "That's pretty good."

"I don't need that," I said. "Really. I'm okay."

Ray's fingers were hurting me, and I knew there'd be bruises on my skin tomorrow.

"We don't think you are," he said.

"I am, I promise," I said. "I'm just afraid of guns."

"All you have to do is hold it," Ray said. "There's not going to be any need to use it."

"Then Pam can do that," I said. "It's her gun."

"I want you to have the fun of it," Pam said. "I can do it another time."

The three of them were watching me. It was clear that I had no choice now but to take the gun and appreciate the honor.

"Okay," I said. "Give it to me."

It was heavier than I'd thought it would be, and as cold as death in my hand.

"The rest of us'll go in first," Ray said. "We'll be in the back of the store in case you need help." He pulled me to him and kissed me, pushing his tongue into my mouth. "For luck," he said.

Pam, Sonny, and Ray got out of the car and went into the Jiffy-Spot. I sat in the front seat shivering and wondered what would happen if I just opened the door and walked away.

I sighed, knowing I'd never have the guts to do that, and got out of the car.

I walked into the Jiffy-Spot with the gun in my hand and my hand in my jacket pocket. I thought the clerk, leaning on the counter over a newspaper, should have been able to tell, with one glance at me, what I was going to do. But he only looked up from his newspaper—somehow I registered that it was in a foreign language—said "Hello," and went back to his reading.

I stopped in front of him and took the gun out of my pocket. He looked up, saw the gun, and, I swear to God, I thought we were both going to faint. Neither of us could say a word.

I don't know how long we might have stood there staring at each other if Mr. Malverne Washington, the night watchman at the building across the street, hadn't forgotten his dinner and come in just then to buy something to eat. It was later that I learned this, of course, and also that he'd played football in high school. High school was a long way back for him, but he'd kept in good shape and when he threw himself on me, I was down for the count.

None of us, the freaked-out clerk, the ferocious Mr. Washington, or me, noticed when Ray, Pam, and Sonny slipped away, but by the time an unnecessary number of cop cars showed up, they were gone and I knew I was taking this fall by myself. I could even hear Pam, all wide-eyed and innocent, telling her father that I must have taken the gun one of those many times I'd been at their house, and her mother sighing and saying that she'd warned Pam about me, but that Pam was just too trusting, too ready to believe in the good in everyone, and as long as she was that way there'd be people like me to take advantage of her.

TWO

I was numb for the trip to the station, and once I got there, I wouldn't answer any questions. There was nothing to deny or explain; I'd been caught in the act, and the last thing I was going to do was to rat on Ray, Pam, and Sonny. They'd never be able to say that I was a fink as well as a loser.

I was sent to Juvenile Hall in a cop cruiser at dawn, still in shock. Still unable to believe that this was really happening to me.

A matron with a hairdo so full of elaborate curls and swoopy waves it looked as if it was the frosting on a wedding cake checked me in, made me take a shower (the bruises from Ray's hand were starting to show), gave me a light-blue jumpsuit and some breakfast, and then opened the door to my cell. It was a regular door, not a barred one, but the window in it assured me there would be no privacy. The floor was cement, the beds were bunks, and the metal sink and toilet were on the back wall, just like in the movies.

And I had a roommate.

She had pale skin and hair dyed so black it looked like crepe paper. The sleeves on her jumpsuit were rolled up so that I could see a swastika tattooed on her upper arm, the muscle of which bulged every time she did a push-up. And she was doing the real kind, not the girl kind, just from the knees up.

"Dahlia," the matron said, "this is Dallas. Dallas, Dahlia. Dallas, you get the top bunk." Then she closed the door and locked it.

Dahlia didn't look at me; she continued pumping out the push-ups. Suddenly she was finished and she sprang to her feet.

"A strong body is imperative to the struggle," she said.

"Struggle?" I said.

"The struggle for the survival of the superior race," she said. "Aren't you concerned about the assault on the white race by the flood of inferior immigrants? And by the black pestilence here at home?"

"Black pestilence?" I asked. What was she talking about?

"The black pestilence," she repeated. "The Negroid race. The so-called African-Americans. If they like Africa so much, they should go back there. That will keep them from sapping the strength of this great and faltering country."

Wonderful, I thought. Bad enough I was in a cell, but I was in one with a racist nut case.

"Oh. Right," I said. I pulled myself up onto the top bunk. "You know, I've been up all night and I think I'll sleep for a while."

"It would be better if you didn't," she said. "Your mind will grow stronger if you can master your physical weaknesses."

"Yeah, well, not today," I said, trying to fluff up the flat pillow. "I'm beat." I closed my eyes. My mind was already busy, thank you very much, trying to master my *mental* weaknesses.

I was alone and I was scared. My father was my only hope for getting out of here in a hurry and I doubted he would be feeling very benevolent toward me just now.

He was definitely not feeling benevolent at my arraignment two days later. He didn't even speak to me. I was surprised nobody else in the courtroom seemed to sense, the way I did, the words "I told you so" coming off him in waves, like an electric current.

I resigned myself to sitting in my cell for three weeks, listening to Dahlia rant and watching her do push-ups until the day of my hearing, when the judge would decide what to do with me. Maybe by then my father would have softened enough to plead for leniency. This was my first offense, after all. Well, not actually my first offense, but the first time I'd been caught at anything.

Dahlia was also waiting for a hearing. She'd tried to force, at knife point, a woman—or, as Dahlia described her, "a person too ignorant to learn the language of the country she had trespassed into"—to give up her seat on a crowded bus to Dahlia.

Our hearings were scheduled for the same day, so there was no chance I'd be getting a better class of criminal for a roommate before I left for wherever I'd be going.

I could receive mail from anybody, though nobody wrote me, but I could only receive calls or visits from family. I didn't get any of those, either. I could call or write anybody I wanted to, so I called Ray every chance I got. I never reached anything but his machine. It made me wonder if he was screening his calls and not answering when he knew it was me. Somehow, I wasn't surprised that he'd do that. I did reach Pam three times, but she didn't have much to say. She was always too busy to talk, running off to do something.

"Where are you going?" I'd ask.

It was the mall, or the coffeehouse, or to meet Sonny at the café. "Wish you were coming, too," she'd say. "Maybe soon."

"Maybe," I'd say. She never mentioned that night, and neither did I, afraid I might be overheard, or that the phone was tapped. We didn't seem to have much to say to each other. I wasn't doing anything but waiting and she was rushing around on vague errands. I hadn't noticed before how much our conversations were about the things we did together; we were either planning what to do or talking about what we'd done.

I didn't call my father or write to him. I wouldn't beg. I wanted him to care enough to come to me.

He never did.

The day of our arraignments, Dahlia and I were escorted to court together.

"Don't expect justice," Dahlia told me. "The system has failed, our citizen's rights have been trampled. We're young and powerless and we have no money; we will be punished."

Apparently she didn't think armed assault or armed robbery were crimes. I had no illusions. I'd done something I knew was bad and I didn't expect I'd get to explain that it wasn't as bad as it looked because my heart wasn't really in it.

My hopes were all pinned on my father. If he would speak up for me, maybe I had a chance. If he would be on my side just this once, I'd make it up to him somehow. Maybe I'd do less skating. For sure, I'd be more careful with the skating I did do. Yeah, he'd been mad at me that last night at home, and he'd never come to see me in Juvie, but he was still my father. He wouldn't want to see me get sent up, would he?

On the way back to Juvenile Hall after the hearing, I needed all my strength to keep from shaking. I could hardly hear Dahlia going on about her Aryan superiority, whatever that was.

"We'll have to be strong," she was saying. "We'll have to resist what our inferiors will try to subject us to."

I wanted to yell at her to shut up. I wanted everything to stop while I tried to figure out what had gone wrong.

My father was there, in the courtroom. We weren't able to talk, but he smiled at me, a calm, pleasant smile which I was stupid enough, or desperate enough, to take for affection. For support.

And then, when the judge said that I could go home on probation if my father thought I could handle it, this being a first offense and all, my father said no. He said that I didn't recognize his authority over me, that I had no respect for any kind of rules, and that I'd be in trouble again before the sheets had been changed on my bunk at Juvie. So the judge gave me six months in the Girls' Rehabilitation Center.

Six months! Three weeks with Dahlia had almost driven me nuts. How was I going to survive six months with her, and with others like her? Yes, Dahlia was going to GRC, too. For the second time. The judge told her this was her last trip there—if she got in trouble again, she'd be going to a work camp. The way he said that made a work camp sound like a place you wanted to make sure you stayed out of.

I don't think I'd even have minded so much going to GRC if I'd known that my father had tried to prevent it. But he was so anxious to get rid of me he'd practically pushed me.

Back at Juvie, the matron with the wedding-cake hairdo escorted us to our cells.

"Well, ladies," she said, throwing a plastic bag on each of our bunks, "I hear you're leaving us. There are the clothes you arrived in. Put them on, leave your coveralls on the bed, and I'll come to get you when it's time to go."

"I can't even remember what I was wearing when I came in here," I said.

"I can," Dahlia said. "And I'll be glad to have it on again."

She stripped off her jumpsuit. "I'm *sick* of this thing," she said, throwing the blue prison uniform onto her bunk. She pulled on black Lycra bike shorts and a black bare-midriff top and stuck big black-and-silver earrings in her earlobes. Her shoes were black combat boots. "God, that feels better," she said, lacing them up. She pulled on her leather jacket. "I was starting to feel like somebody else in those droopy drawers."

I was, too. Maybe that was the point of jailhouse uniforms. Just like the boredom was probably supposed to do something to you, too. All it did to me was make me understand why cons ended up writing books that made no sense or spent hours on bodybuilding, or just got meaner and crazier.

"How long do most people get?" I asked as I changed, wanting to know where I ranked on the scale of juvenile criminals.

"Three to nine months is usual. Last time, I got three."

If Dahlia was the result of three months of rehabilitation, I hated to think what she'd be like after six. And the fact that she'd gotten only three months the first time made me wonder what the judge saw when he looked at me to give me six.

The guard returned. "Okay, Dallas and Dahlia," she said. "Time to go. Your limo's leaving now."

A white van with the city seal on the door waited in the driveway. In it were a driver, an armed attendant, and a black girl with a scabby lower lip and a right eye that was swollen shut. The girl wore jeans, a plain green sweatshirt, and a purple satin jacket.

Before I got into the van, the matron put one hand on my arm and one on Dahlia's and said, "Let's not see you back here again, okay? Use your chance. You've got a lot of years ahead of you. Make them ones you're proud of, okay, girls?"

Neither of us looked at her before we got into the van. Six months' incarceration was a *chance*? A chance for what? To learn how to be a better criminal was all I could think of.

The beaten-up black girl never said a word, never even moved for the whole twenty-minute drive. Just kept her hands in her lap and her eyes on her hands.

THREE

At Girls' Rehab we were unloaded under guard and taken inside. A compactly built blond woman with a militarily short haircut met us. She took us into an office, where we sat in metal chairs.

"My name's Connie," she said. "I'm one of the daytime probation officers who'll be watching out for you. The girls here usually call us p.o.'s or coaches. Which one of you is Dahlia, the one who's been here before?"

Dahlia jerked her chin up.

"You know the rules, then," Connie said. "But it won't hurt for you to hear them again." She read a long list of rules to us. About the only thing we could do without asking was breathing. No arguing, no insulting anyone, no talking in the halls, no profanity, no talking about our crimes, present or past, no touching, no food in the rooms, no sharing food at meals, no letters to people in penal institutions, no guns or glue or aerosol cans, no alcohol or gum or Satanism. We had to wear pajamas or nightgowns and sleep between the sheets. We had to have permission to leave our rooms. We would be searched after we had visitors. We had to wear bras and shoes except in the shower or in bed. And a million other things, plus the demerits and penalties if we broke any of the rules.

"I know you can't remember all this," Connie said. "You'll each get a booklet with everything written down. Saying 'I didn't know I couldn't do that' will not be permitted as an excuse. Have the rules stayed about the same since you were here before, Dahlia?"

Dahlia shrugged and said nothing.

"An answer is required," Connie said.

Dahlia glowered at her and said shortly, "Yes."

"Everybody who leaves here says they're never coming back," Connie said. "They all mean it at the time. As you can see, it doesn't always work out that way." She turned to the black girl. "You're Damaris?" The girl nodded, looking at the floor. "He did you pretty good, didn't he?"

Damaris's head went up and down once.

"But you still love him, right?"

Damaris was silent. Her head came up slightly, as if she was going to nod again, and then stopped when she caught on that maybe "yes" was the wrong answer this time.

"Enough to run his dope for him. Put yourself in the way for him. Take his bad temper. And don't try to tell me he didn't have you doing his drugs, too. Because sometimes he's good to you, right? You listen to me, Damaris, you won't have to take any more of that ever again once you leave here. Not if you don't want to."

Damaris said nothing.

"Dallas," she said, turning her attention to me. "It's a mistake you're here?" When I started to answer, she held up her hand. "Never mind. It's always a mistake. Nobody in here ever thinks

SKIDMORE COLLEGE LIBRARY

she ought to be. Everybody's part of the Brady Bunch, and the criminal justice system is totally messed up, harassing innocent folks and believing that all teenagers want to do is make trouble. I've heard it a thousand times."

I stiffened at being so misjudged. I *knew* I'd committed a crime. I was caught in the act, there were witnesses, there was no denying it, even if I still thought being able to explain why I'd done it might have made a difference in my sentence. But I'd just been told I wasn't supposed to argue and I wasn't supposed to talk about my crime. Was Connie trying to trick me into breaking a rule before I'd been here an hour?

She shuffled through our papers and went on. "You'll learn that I'm your mother, your sister, your warden, your confessor, whatever you want me to be and some things you don't. My job is to help you clean up so when you get out of here you don't have a chance of coming back." She laughed, short and harsh. "There are days when I still believe that. Maybe one of you will be the girl who actually does it. Okay. The others are at lunch now, but we don't like to bring in new girls during meals. Class time is better. Come on. You need rooms and lunch and some clothes and supplies for you, Dahlia. You know you can't wear those clothes in here."

"Friends of Felons is going to dress me again?" she asked.

"They're not called Friends of Felons and you know it," Connie said. "You should be grateful there's a volunteer group that takes enough interest in you all to want to help you when the only clothes some of you have are inappropriate for GRC."

"They're just a bunch of rich and pampered parasites who like to shop," Dahlia said. "Buying stuff for us is an excuse for them to go spend money on outfits I wouldn't wear on the outs at gunpoint."

"Well, you're not wearing that Biker Mama outfit here," Connie said. "How you look influences how you behave and how you see yourself."

"That's what you think," Dahlia muttered.

Connie led us across a large room with easy chairs and couches, a Ping-Pong table, bookshelves, a desk where a woman sat writing in a folder. We went through a door that opened into a corridor with rooms on each side of it.

"Anybody want a single room? We've got one available. How about you, Damaris?"

Damaris shook her head and spoke for the first time. Her voice was quiet and sweet in an innocent way. "I never slept in a room by myself."

"Okay," Connie said. "Dahlia?"

"I'd prefer it," Dahlia said.

Connie opened a door and showed Dahlia in. It was a tiny room with a bed, a small chest of drawers, and a chair. There was a doorless closet in one corner and a barred window over the bed.

"The Presidential Suite," Connie said. "Make yourself at home. I'll be back." She closed the door and we went on down the hall. "I think I'll put you in here, Damaris. With Valencia."

She opened a door into a room exactly twice as big as Dahlia's, with two of everything that Dahlia's room had. One side of the room was clearly unused. The bed on the other side had a stuffed tiger on the pillow, photographs taped to the wall over the dresser, and clothes hanging in the open closet.

"Valencia's fifteen, same as you, Damaris," Connie told her.

"Yeah?" Damaris said, and sat down on the unused bed.

"I'll be back," Connie told Damaris.

She took me to the end of the hall. "You get our last vacancy.

Lucky for you. If we don't have enough beds, you have to sleep at Juvie and come over here during the day for school and meals. It can be inconvenient."

As if being here wasn't already inconvenient.

"Your roommate is Shatasia. All those pictures on the bureau are of her little girl."

"How old is she?" I asked.

"About a year and a half, I think. Cute, isn't she?"

"No. I meant Shatasia."

"Oh. She was just seventeen. We had her birthday party in the common room last week."

Seventeen. That meant her baby was born when she was fifteen and a half. That meant she'd gotten pregnant when she was fourteen. I couldn't imagine what that would be like. I didn't even like babies. They were always drooling or barfing or crying or smelling bad. Hard enough to take if you were grown up and wanted one. How would it feel to know you'd be getting one at fourteen?

"Is somebody bringing you your things?" Connie asked.

"My father."

"I'll be on the lookout for him. And I'll bring you some lunch. Normally, there's no food allowed in the rooms, but you'll need to eat something before you go to class. We don't want you to fall behind. Any further behind than you already are," she added.

"What makes you think I'm behind?" I asked. "You think I'm stupid or something?"

"No," Connie said mildly. "But, let's face it, most criminals are not honor students. But don't let that stop you from being one. Are you?"

"I could be," I muttered. Well, I *could* be, I told myself. I hadn't done much in school for a long time, but if I wanted to, I probably could have done okay. School was kind of like robbing a Jiffy-Spot: no matter how much you wanted everything to go right, you couldn't count on that. Things happened that messed you up so much you couldn't go back and get straightened out. After you'd skipped a certain number of classes you were lost, and then there was almost no point in even trying.

Connie left. I went to look at the pictures of Shatasia's little girl. She was cute, and I'm not one who thinks all babies are cute. There are plenty of butt-ugly babies around. This one was chubby and smily, with a lot of little pigtails. In one picture she had on socks with lace around the edges, and in another one she had on pink-and-white striped overalls with a matching hat. She looked like somebody had been fussing over her. In none of my few baby pictures did I look as well-groomed as this baby.

Connie returned with a tray: vegetable soup and a sub sandwich, orange juice and a banana. She left it, saying she'd come for me in about half an hour, in time for class.

This food was a thousand times better than the stuff they served us at Juvie. I took my time, enjoying the meal. Before I finished, Connie came back.

"Your father's here with your things," she said.

I put the banana on my pillow and got up.

"No food in the rooms," she said.

"But I just had *lunch* in my room. I want to save my banana for later," I said. Did they write rules just for the fun of making us bad girls obey them, rules that had no reasons except to make sure we knew who were the bosses and who were the vermin?

"I'll keep it for you," she said. "You can have it whenever you want it. The reason we don't want food in the rooms is that it gives some girls one more thing to fight about or to steal, or to make messes with."

Anger came up in me like a flood. I didn't want to steal anybody else's banana, or make a mess with one, but I did want to fight for *this* banana. It was *mine* and so little else now was. Why should I need someone else to keep it for me? Why couldn't I have something private, even if it was only a banana?

Sullenly, as if it was a loaded weapon, I handed the banana over.

My father was sitting in the visiting room with a suitcase beside him.

"Dallas," he said, standing when I came in.

I didn't speak.

He watched me without trying to touch me. Then he said, "I hope I brought everything you need. I'm sure you'll tell me if I forgot anything."

I still didn't speak, just looked off over his shoulder.

He sat down. "I know you're angry at me. And I know you don't want to be in here. But think about this. What would you be doing if you'd been allowed to go home?"

I hated it when he said, "Think about this." He said it all the time, and what it meant was: Think about how right I am and how wrong you are. Like that was something I might really do.

He went on. "You'd be back out there by tonight, getting in more trouble."

I kept looking past him, mentally yawning. I knew these sermons by heart.

"You need a lesson, Dallas. You need something to wake you up."

"I'll tell you the lesson I learned," I said, looking straight at him. "My own father couldn't be bothered to stick up for me."

"I hope someday you'll see that what I did was for your own good. You won't listen to me or do what I ask you to. Maybe in here you can learn something."

"Learn what? My roommate for the past three weeks was a genuine nut case, not that you ever bothered to find that out, and I'm sure there are more of them in here. What am I supposed to learn from them? You just want me out of your way so you don't have to be bothered with me."

He stood up. "Let me know if I've forgotten anything you need. I'll be back on visitors' day."

"Don't bother," I said. "I don't want to see you. And don't try to pretend that you want to see me. I know what you think."

"You do? And what is that?"

"You resent Dixie Lee for dying and leaving you stuck with me. So you resent me, too. I've always been more trouble than I was worth, some chore you can't get out of doing, like cleaning the garage forever or something. I'm too much like her and not enough like what you wanted. You wish you'd never had me."

"I can't talk about this now," he said.

"You'll never talk about it," I retorted. "But it's still true."

His face worked as if he was going to cry. Or scream at me. Then he threw up his hands and said, "Okay. I *did* resent your mother's dying. She made a fool of me. But I had you to raise and I took the job seriously. More seriously than she did, that's for sure. I bathed you every day and dressed you in clean clothes. I made you decent meals, even if they were frozen. I got you to school on time. I was holding down a job, too, don't forget. And I was determined you weren't going to be like her, pleasing only yourself and having no regard for anybody around you. Well, I failed at that. I don't know why. Maybe it was because you missed having a mother, even one like her. Maybe I didn't laugh enough or buy you the right kind of sneakers. Who knows? But you're the one who's gotten herself into this place and you're the one who'll have to take the consequences for what you've done. I'm through. I've had all I can take from you. If being on your own is what you want, then you've got it." He looked at me for a moment, then turned and left.

I stood, watching him go, stunned. Sure, he'd spent plenty of time in the past lecturing me, questioning me, punishing me, begging me to improve my behavior, but somehow, though he'd threatened it before, I never believed he'd really abandon me. He may not have liked what I'd done—he may not have liked *me*—but he was my father. Like he said, he'd taken the job seriously. *Too* seriously, I often thought.

Had he found out about all the things I'd shoplifted? Did he know I'd sneaked out after he was asleep to be with Pam or Ray? To drink stolen six-packs, or to scare lone pedestrians on dark streets? Was the Jiffy-Spot robbery the final straw? Or was it the only thing he knew about for sure and it was just too big for him?

After a moment, I straightened my shoulders and picked up my suitcase.

As I put it on the bed in my room, Connie came to the door. "Since you've just had a visitor, I'll need to search you and your suitcase before we go get Dahlia and Damaris to go to class."

FOUR

The classroom was big and bright, with pictures on the wall under a banner that said WOMEN WHO MADE A DIFFERENCE. The only one I recognized was Eleanor Roosevelt. A few girls sat at their desks with books or papers, but most were wandering around the room, apparently doing nothing. They all stopped to stare at the three of us when we came in. They probably always stared at new girls, but Dahlia, with her crepe-paper hair, button-down shirt, and dirndl skirt, was an especially interesting study in style.

I wondered which one was Shatasia.

Connie took us to the teacher. "Kate, this is Damaris, Dahlia, and Dallas. I guess you'll be seeing in 3-D today."

The teacher laughed. "Hi, girls," she said. "3-D is right. I'll work with each of you individually later to see where you are in your studies, but for right now take some paper and a pencil and sit down. We're about to start our daily writing assignment. Why don't the three of you sit in the front here?"

We did as we were told. Kate clapped her hands and, when no one paid any attention, put her fingers in her mouth and whistled. It was something I'd always wanted to know how to do. "Hey!" she said. "Everybody sit down. We've got some new people today. This is Damaris." She held her hand over Damaris's head. "Dahlia. And Dallas. The 3-Ds. Now take your seats, please. I'll put the writing topic on the board and, as usual, I'd prefer you write about that, but if you have some strong objection, just pick your own topic and write. I'd rather have you write about *something* than not write at all."

She turned to the board and wrote as the wandering girls drifted into seats. Still jarred by my father's reaction, I hoped nothing but indifference showed on my face. I needed to find a way to feel strong again, to be in control. I distracted myself by checking Kate out. She was probably in her mid- to late thirties, tall and straight, with short dark hair as smooth and shiny as calm water. She wore a red sweater, a plaid pleated skirt, and flat red shoes. She looked like a suburban mom in a movie-of-the-week. So why would she want to be teaching a roomful of criminals?

When she turned from the board, I saw that she'd written *When was the last time you cried? Why?*

"Okay, you have twenty minutes. Go!"

I was supposed to write about *that*? I thought she'd have us writing about how we were going to be good from now on, or about what we did last summer.

But the question made me think. When *had* I last cried? I felt like it sometimes at the movies, or during certain sappy TV commercials. And at other times, too, when I couldn't even say why. But tears seemed so useless. I couldn't see the point of them, or how they fixed anything that was wrong. Besides, the idea of crying made me feel weak and incompetent, ways I didn't like to feel.

I searched my memory. When?

I slid my eyes sideways and saw on Damaris's paper, in an elaborate script with curlicues under the words, *"Last night."* Sliding my eyes the other way, to Dahlia's paper, I read, written in a heavy up-and-down hand, *"Crying is for babies."* Apparently, Dahlia and I had something in common after all.

Finally, I wrote: *I can't remember when I last cried. Why bother? Crying never changes anything and it gives you a headache. A girl at school told me once that if you don't cry, all your tears back up and make a pool inside you until someday, maybe when it's very inconvenient, you'll have to cry. I don't know whether to believe that or not. If you ever do feel like you're going to cry, you can stop it by squeezing the bridge of your nose and looking up, like you're trying to see the top of your head.*

I looked at what I'd written. How many times had I stopped myself from crying? Somehow I knew what I'd written about squeezing your nose and looking up was true and that I'd done it, but I couldn't actually remember. When?

"Time," Kate called, and walked among the desks, collecting the papers. "For you new girls, the 3-Ds, we write every day and the papers go into your folder. It makes a kind of journal for you, to take with you when you leave. I correct spelling and punctuation and grammar, but the content is just between you and me. Okay, I want the X math group to work on Chapter 9 in the red book and the Z group in the blue book on Chapter 11 while I get these Ds fixed up."

Nobody seemed to pay much attention to her. Of the thirty or so girls in the room, only a few actually pulled out books. The rest put their heads down on their desks, or talked to each other, or were on their feet again, wandering.

While I waited my turn with Kate, I watched the other girls, who watched me back. I never let my eyes be the first to turn away.

I listened to them talk. Some of them spoke Spanish and some spoke English in that fast, hip, street way that sounded so cool. I wondered what they'd all done to be here.

Some caught my interest more than others. There was a tall, gangly, painfully thin black girl who wandered around with her hand on her concave stomach. Two Hispanic girls looked at a *National Geographic* together, making comments in Spanish. They both had mountains of black hair, but one of them had a sweet face and a *Playboy* centerfold body, while the other—I heard someone call her Sylviana—sported a red streak in the front of her hair and gang tattoos on the knuckles of her muscular hands. She wore a high-necked white blouse and plaid slacks that seemed so unlikely a style for her I wondered if she, too, was being dressed by Friends of Felons. Another girl, whose notebook had TOOZDAE written on the front in fat, overlapping letters, was so pale and fair-haired that she looked almost transparent. She seemed too young and frail to be capable of doing anything she could have gotten in trouble for.

"Hey!" Kate said, sending Dahlia and Damaris back to their seats with some kind of assignments. "Settle down now and get to work. You want to have some smarts when you're on the outs, don't you?" She waited a minute, watching the girls settle themselves, and then said, "Okay, Dallas, your turn." I went to her desk and sat in the chair beside hers. "Have you been going to school?" she asked me.

"Yes. Sometimes."

"You're what? A junior?"

I nodded.

"And how have you been doing?"

I shrugged. "Not great."

Kate methodically questioned me about my grades and my classes and said, "I can see you haven't been working up to your potential, but there's nothing wrong with your brain. Not like some of the other girls who've messed theirs up with too many drugs. Maybe in here, with fewer distractions, you can concentrate better. Do you like to read?"

"Well, I *can* read, if that's what you mean," I said, so keyed up that almost anything could sound like an insult.

"It's not," Kate said, handing me a math book with an assignment written on a piece of paper and a paperback book. "You might find this interesting," she said. "I didn't read it until I was in college, but I wish I'd known about it sooner."

The book was called *The Member of the Wedding*. I had never heard of it. It was by somebody named Carson McCullers and I didn't know if that was a man or a woman.

"Okay, you guys," Kate said. "Get ready for P-E. Put your things away. Don't forget, essays on 'Is Breaking and Entering a Good Career Choice?' are due tomorrow. You 3-Ds are excused from that one since everybody's supposed to have been working on it for a week."

The girls slammed noisily around, putting books back on shelves, finding jackets, and getting themselves into a rough line at the door.

Connie appeared and led us outside. "Volleyball today," she said. "Nobody on bed rest, so we'll have good teams. Count off. Ones on that side of the net, twos on this side."

A big black girl with strong-looking calves and slicked-back hair gathered into a knob at the back of her neck immediately took charge of my team, which included Dahlia and Toozdae, the transparent-looking girl.

"Okay," the big black girl said. "You"—she pointed at Dahlia—"can serve. Toozdae, go there. You at the net . . ." And pointing around, she distributed us. All of us except Dahlia went where we were told to. I heard another black girl on the team mutter under her breath, "Shatasia, you are bossy to the bone."

Knowing how Dahlia felt about what she called the Black Pestilence, I watched her watching Shatasia.

Shatasia noticed Dahlia standing at the sideline. She put her hands on her hips. "Well, come on, girl. We got us a game to win here."

"Who put you in charge?" Dahlia asked.

All the other girls stopped talking at once and watched, as alert as forest animals sensing a predator.

Shatasia's eyes opened wider and then narrowed. "I didn't see nobody else steppin' up," she said. "You got a problem with that?"

"Yes," Dahlia said. "No one tells me what to do. Especially not someone like you."

Connie watched but didn't move. Only her eyes swept back and forth from the face-off between Shatasia and Dahlia to the rest of us: back and forth, back and forth.

"Hey, girl," Shatasia said, and her knees bent slightly as if she was getting ready to spring. "How's this game supposed to start if nobody be's the leader? Huh? You tell me."

"Nobody inferior to me gives me orders," Dahlia said, staring Shatasia down.

Shatasia took a step toward Dahlia. "You sayin' I'm inferior to you?" Her legs shook visibly with some terrible effort. It was impossible to tell if she was getting ready to jump on Dahlia or trying not to.

Connie stepped in. "You're out of line, Dahlia. Nobody's superior to anybody else in here except me because I get to go home at night. I'm giving you twenty-four hours' room confinement, and if anything like this happens again, there'll be a heavier penalty. You're supposed to be learning something besides street behavior." She turned to Shatasia. "Congratulations, Shatasia. You showed good control."

"You thought I was goin' to go for her, didn't you?" Shatasia asked, grinning.

"Were you?" Connie asked.

"Well, I tell you, I was trying not to, but I don't know how long I could have resisted."

"Then it's good I stepped in. But let's keep thinking you'd have settled it with words and not physically." She looked around. "Good job, the rest of you, for staying out of it. I'm proud of all of you."

Connie took Dahlia's arm, and Dahlia wrenched it away.

"Don't touch me," she said, and stalked in through the doors to the common room, her chin up.

Kate clapped her hands. "Okay, let's play volleyball. Get ready."

Shatasia turned to us, her team, and smiled, a great toothy, triumphant smile. "Now, you *ladies*, if y'all don't *mind*, how about taking your places so we can kick some serious butt here."

FIVE

After the game, which we won, Connie lined us up to go in. "Fifteen minutes to clean up and then group. If you're excused from group, I want to see your pass and know the reason why. It's Monday, so today is AA."

I washed my hands and spent the rest of my fifteen minutes at the common-room doors, looking out to the P-E yard and wondering how hard it would be to get over the wall, and where I would go if I could get out.

"It's possible," Connie said behind me. "This place isn't escape-proof by a long shot. But you know you'll get picked up again, don't you?"

"Why should I?" I asked, without turning to face her.

"Because the kind of person who'll run is the kind who'll commit more crimes. If you want to clean up, you stay here and learn how."

I didn't answer, just kept measuring the height of the wall with my eyes.

"Turning around's easier now than it will be in a few years. Or in a lot of years."

"If you want to turn around," I said.

"That's right," Connie answered before she walked off. "If you want to."

In AA I sat and listened to other girls talk about drinking. I had the feeling they were saying what they knew they were supposed to say, not what they were really thinking. I may not be as good a liar as Pam, but I knew how to work that con, too. I didn't believe the ones who said they knew they wouldn't drink anymore, that it caused them too many problems. Even when you knew that, even when you were driving drunk and knew you shouldn't be, there was still a good part to the buzz. Only when you were sick from it did drinking seem like a bad idea, and you always promised yourself you'd stop before you got that far the next time.

After an hour of fairy-tale atonements, the group broke up and went in different directions, to do homework, nap, write letters, who knew what. Maybe to plan escapes.

In my room, I unpacked the suitcase my father had brought. He'd done an okay job of packing for me. Why wouldn't he? He wanted every trace of me out of his house. He'd even bought me new bottles of shampoo, conditioner, and hand lotion. Sort of farewell presents, I supposed.

I hung up my clothes and put them in drawers. I didn't care what I looked like in here. Except if Ray came to see me. Then it would matter.

I'd write him again. Tell him where I was and that I needed to see him. I'd do that after dinner. Right now, I was tired.

I sat on my bed with my chin on my chest for quite a while, looking at *The Member of the Wedding* lying at the foot of the bed. My head jerked up as Shatasia came through the door.

"Well, hallelujah it's you and not that Dahlia goin' to be my roomie. That would have been some fun, don't you think?"

"Dahlia wanted the single room."

"Good idea." Shatasia kissed her fingertip and pressed it onto the picture of her baby. "This is my Sharly. Ain't she the cutest thing you ever saw?"

"Yeah. She's real cute."

"She's with my grandma. Gram comes every Tuesday night and Sunday afternoon so Sharly don't forget me. I sure do miss her."

"She's real cute," I said again.

"My grandma's taking good care of her," Shatasia went on. "She always looks nice and clean and happy. Gram's good with babies. It's just when they get older she don't know what to do with them, how to keep them out of trouble. That's a hard thing to do."

"Hard enough to do even for yourself. Supposing it's something you want in the first place."

Shatasia laughed. "That's right, girl. You right. Bein' good can be a snooze. What's your name again?"

"Dallas Carpenter."

"I'm Shatasia Jefferson. Shatasia M'Tafi Jefferson. That's a beautiful name, right? My mama didn't have much she could give me, so she made sure I'd have something beautiful for my whole life. I did that for my Sharly, too. Her whole name's Sharlotta Krisha T'Raina Jefferson. And she's going to have more for her life than just a pretty name."

"What else will she have?" I asked.

"She's going to have a home that's happy and that's safe." Shatasia sat on her bed with Sharly's photograph in her hands. "Won't be no men comin' into her bedroom when she's too young to know how to protect herself. Won't be no guns in my house, and no drugs, either. And she's going to have a mama who never leaves her again."

"Sounds good," I said.

"And she's going to stay in school and not have no babies until she's married. She's going to do right all the things I did wrong. She's going to be *happy*." Shatasia's eyes glittered. I could have told her to squeeze her nose and look up, but she didn't need my help. She kissed Sharly's picture and put it back on the bureau. "What you in here for, Dallas? I'm not suppose to ask you that. Rules say we not suppose to talk about our deeds, just like we not suppose to do almost everything, but what they think we are? Girl Scouts? Sure we talk about our deeds."

There was no point in keeping it a secret. Sooner or later I knew I'd tell. Might as well be sooner. Anyway, I was curious to know what Shatasia had done. I'd show her mine if she'd show me hers. "Armed robbery. A Jiffy-Spot. But my biggest crime is stupidity. I got caught."

Shatasia giggled. "Oh, girl, all of us here could get the chair for stupidity. We all really good at it. How about those other people? They get caught, too?"

"What other people?"

"You didn't do it alone, did you?"

"Why not?" Did I appear too dumb to do a job by myself?

"That's not the kind of thing gets done alone," Shatasia said. She understood crimes, that much was plain.

I blew out a breath. "You're right," I said. "But I'm the one who got nailed."

Shatasia giggled again. "We all sure got a lot to thank our homies for, don't we? Get us in trouble and then take off. Same with me. I was in a gang bomb on the bus. A bunch of us ran into a bunch of them. They started mad-dogging us, and we was mad-dogging back, but it didn't stop there—does it ever?—and pretty soon we had to run up or shut up, with weapons, too. I got mopped pretty bad. When the transit cops came, everybody split but me and Monique. She was here, too, but she made too much trouble, so they sent her to a camp. Me, I'm cleanin' up. It's just luck Sharly wasn't with me on that bus."

"You had a weapon?" I asked. Buses were chancy places to be—more than I'd realized. Shatasia and Dahlia both were here for bus-related sins.

"Girlfriend, I *always* had a weapon. I never felt safe for a minute without my little .22."

"Did you ever use it?"

"Oh, yeah. I shot it a few times, doin' drive-bys. Never hit anybody that I know about, but I could have. It was good to have to make myself look down and crazy. How else you gonna get some respect? How 'bout you? What you carry?"

"I've never had a gun."

"What about the 'armed' part of that robbery?"

"It was somebody else's. She gave it to me, but later she said I stole it."

"Oooh," Shatasia said. "Guess you'll be settin' things straight with her one of these days."

A buzzer sounded in the hall.

"What's that for?" I asked.

"Dinner. After that we got jobs, and prep time for homework, and showers. Then in rooms by nine for bedtime stories, and lights out at ten. I know it's wacked, but I kinda like that, knowin' what's goin' to happen next even if I don't always want to do it. But most of these freaks, they hate it. There's way too many rules, I agree with that, but I still like to know what's happenin' next. Most of the time."

Rules reminded me of my banana. It had seemed so important at lunchtime, and then I'd forgotten all about it.

Dinner was good: meatloaf, mashed potatoes, and peas, with apple crisp for dessert. Before Juvie, I hadn't had what you'd call a home-cooked meal in a long time. Defrosting was my father's specialty. Besides, I didn't like eating with him because the side dish was always a lecture about my conduct. Mostly I stayed away from home, eating fast food while I watched parents and their kids putting away burgers and fries and playing with the plastic giveaway toys. I liked watching them, even when they fought or whined. They looked safe inside their little families, sure of their places, connected.

I drew the job of washing the tables after they'd been cleared. It was an easy job, and fast; hardly a job at all. I even wiped down each chair, too, to make it take a little longer before I had to go out into the common room with everyone else. I was tired and on serious overload. It was good to leave my brain turned off for a while.

When I'd washed everything I could wash, I got paper and an envelope from Barbara, one of the night coaches, and sat on a couch in front of the TV to write to Ray. The thin black girl with her hand on her stomach sat at the other end of the couch.

"They won't let us watch anything good," she said. "No MTV or anything like that."

"Yeah?" I said. "How come?"

"They think it gives us bad ideas. Like we can't think of them by ourselves."

"Maybe they're afraid we'll want to become rock stars," I said.

The girl laughed. "Yeah. That's probably it. Those rock stars. They cause a lot of trouble. What's your name again?"

"Dallas. Like in Texas."

"Hi. I'm Lolly. Like in pop." She laughed again.

"You been here long?"

"Couple weeks. Only eight and a half months to go. How long you here for?"

"Six months."

"Guess I'm worse than you, then," Lolly said. "How many times you get picked up before they finally took you in?"

"Never," I said.

"You're kidding me," Lolly exclaimed. "Everybody else here, the cops stopped them lots of times before they finally got arrested. It's good, being a girl. They give you warnings and let you go more often than they do the guys. You sure you never got stopped? Not even once?"

"Never," I said again.

"So the first time, bam! You must have got nailed with a gun in your hand or something."

"Bingo," I said.

"Yeah?" Lolly sat up straighter. "Armed robbery? Assault with a deadly weapon? That's me. Assault. Except I had a knife. A Quicksilver with an AM6 utility blade and a stainless-steel handle with a thumb knob. Folds up to nothing. Cost me fifty bucks, but I guess I won't be getting it back."

"I wouldn't count on it."

"Barbara's giving me the evil eye. I got to go do my homework. I'm going to see if she'll let me have some popcorn while I work. You want some? I'm starving."

She sure looked like she was. "No thanks. I'm full from dinner."

Lolly wandered away.

I wrote my letter to Ray. It didn't take long. Then I did the math assignment Kate had given me. It didn't take long either. I was surprised I remembered enough to be able to do the problems. Maybe I *would* concentrate better here. Who would believe it?

The two dark-haired girls did their homework together, speaking in machine-gun Spanish that made them sound like they were planning an invasion. It was only a question of time before they sent Dahlia into overdrive about us Aryans and how we were the only ones capable of ever being excellent and how people of color shouldn't be allowed in so that they could sap our great and faltering country, etc., etc., etc. I'd soaked up more of her ranting than I'd realized.

Shatasia bent over her work, pressing hard with her pencil, intent and serious. Toozdae twiddled with her pale hair, tapped her pencil, and seemed to be thinking of something else.

Damaris stared into space, touching her split lip and her swollen eye and looking as if she was going to cry.

After a while, a buzzer sounded. A thin, sharp-featured woman with a new, too-tight perm and eyebrows penciled straight across rose from behind the desk before the buzzer had even stopped. "Showers," she said. "Go to your room to get ready, or there'll be no bedtime stories."

We began closing our books and gathering up our papers. Damaris jumped up and headed straight for the hall to the bedrooms. Everyone seemed to be doing what she was supposed to be doing, but the thin woman raised her voice. "No fooling around. You little hoods take advantage every chance you get, but you better not try anything with me."

I looked around to see who she was talking to, but didn't see anybody breaking any of the million and a half rules.

"I know how your minds work," the thin woman said.

"Who's that?" I asked the girl walking next to me. She was one of the Spanish-speaking girls, Sylviana, the tough-looking one with the red streak in her hair and the tattoos.

"Her name's Mary Alice," she said in perfect unaccented English. "She's one of the night coaches. She comes on when Connie leaves."

"Sylviana," Mary Alice said, "you and the new girl shut up and get ready for showers."

Sylviana lowered her voice. "She hates us and it's more than mutual. We call her Malice and she deserves it."

I went into my room and Shatasia came in right behind me.

"How you like Malice?" she asked, closing the door behind us. "Pretty low, ain't she?"

"She sure seems annoyed about something."

"Annoyed ain't the half of it," Shatasia said. "She's got some kind of serious attitude problem. Hurry now and get ready for showers or she'll turn off our story. We got to be finished in six minutes, shampoos and everything."

I started getting undressed. "You mean *real* bedtime stories? I thought 'bedtime stories' was slang for something in here, like getting in bed on time or something."

"No, it's real bedtime stories," she said. "Like I'm gonna read to my Sharly when I'm on the outs."

"You mean," I said, pulling on a bathrobe I'd never worn at home, "somebody tells us stories?"

Shatasia took the elastic from her hair and combed it out. "Volunteers, they come at night and read on the P-A system. Every room's got a separate control switch, and if you've been bad that day, you get your switch turned off and you don't get the story. So you better not cause us to get our switch flipped, cause I love those stories. Now hurry up. We got to be showered, changed, and in the bed before the stories start."

We weren't allowed to speak as we stood in line in the steamy shower room, waiting for our turns. Buzzers went off signaling the beginning and the end of six minutes, and girls wrapped in towels hustled into the locker room to dry off, while the next batch of girls went into the water. All the while, Malice kept hollering.

"Keep moving! No talking! Hurry up! Come on, you little tramps, get going! You want demerits? You want punishment? Valencia, you may think you've got a hot body, but none of us want to see it. Get covered up!"

She didn't stop the whole time we were showering, and the echo off the tiles made her even harder to take.

"What is her problem?" I asked Shatasia, once we were back in our room.

"I got my theories," she said. "But not now. It's story time." She buttoned up her pajamas and was plumping the pillow behind her.

I got into bed and lay on my back, not knowing what to expect. Shatasia turned Sharly's picture on the dresser so she could see it, and she sat, holding a stuffed rabbit in her lap. "Sharly's got a bunny just like this," she said. "It makes me feel close to her, to know every night we're huggin' the same bunny. Almost like I was huggin' her."

The lights in the room dimmed and some music came over

43

the intercom. It was classical, I knew that much, but I didn't know what kind. It was nice.

Then a voice began to read, a grandmotherly sort of voice, warm and quiet.

"In the High and Far-Off Times," she began, "the Elephant, O Best Beloved, had no trunk . . ."

I looked across at Shatasia. Her eyes were closed and she was smiling.

The words of the story were both formal and intimate, and the rhythm of them was lulling. I couldn't remember anybody reading me a bedtime story before.

When she was finished, the grandmotherly reader told us the story was by Rudyard Kipling and was called "The Elephant's Child." In it, the Elephant's Child got spanked by his relatives every time he asked a question, even when he asked them most politely to stop. It was no surprise to me that, when he got his trunk, he went home and spanked them all with it for a long time.

Were we supposed to identify with the vengeful Elephant's Child, or were we supposed to learn from the relatives to be nicer to each other? I didn't get the message.

Then the grandmotherly voice read a poem about a canoe on a lake, with the paddle dipping, dipping, dipping—

SIX

The next thing I knew, it was morning and the six-thirty buzzer was going off.

"I swear to God, that thing is going to give me a heart attack one of these days," Shatasia said, sitting up in bed.

My own heart was pounding in alarm. It took a long, disoriented moment for me to remember where I was. Not home. Not Juvie. Where?

"Fire drills are worse," Shatasia went on. "They're always at two A.M. in the morning. Come on, it's good to be first in the bathroom, so you don't have to wait. If you come in after Valencia or Sylviana, you never get in front of a mirror. They can spend a week doin' their hair."

I followed Shatasia to the bathroom, where a p.o. waited outside the door, watching us.

On the way back to our room, I said, "It smelled like somebody'd been sick in there."

"Oh, that's probably just Lolly, barfin' up whatever she eats. She's not the only one does that. Lots of girls gain weight here, cause they're eatin' regular and not doin' drugs, and they don't like gettin' fat. But Lolly's the worst. Couple or more times a day. Ugh! Can you even *think* about doin' that?"

I shook my head. "Is that allowed here? It seems like hardly anything else is."

"Never heard anybody say it wasn't. But how you gonna stop somebody wants to do that?"

"Well, what happens now? Breakfast?"

"Clothes first. You have to get dressed every morning, even if you're on bed rest."

"What's that?"

"If you're sick, or you got cramps. Like that, you know. Breakfast, jobs, school, lunch, school, P-E, group, free time, dinner, jobs, prep time, showers, bed. They're tryin' to teach us to get organized. But once in a while I just want to sleep till noon, have fries and Baby Ruths for dinner, cut school. You know, like a vacation."

"I'd like to do all that right now," I said.

Shatasia laughed. "But we'd better get dressed instead. I don't want no demerits that'll keep me from havin' visitors or bedtime stories, or from gettin' my weekend furloughs when I get closer to finishin' my sentence."

"Do people ever escape from here?" I asked casually.

"Oh, yeah." Shatasia was puzzling between two T-shirts. "All the time. It's not that hard. But they almost always get caught. Sometimes they get sent to the camp. Sometimes they come back here. Cause, you know, they don't leave here with the idea that they're goin' to do better in school and quit hangin' with their homies." She picked the green T-shirt. Then she looked at me. "You could do it if you wanted."

I said nothing, just went on dressing. But I was thinking. Thinking about getting out of here, and what I'd do if I could. My father wouldn't help me. Would Pam? Would Ray? If they wouldn't, where would I go? What would I do?

"What is *group*, anyway?" I asked Shatasia as we made our beds and dusted and vacuumed our room after breakfast. "Is there something besides AA?"

"It's different things they think we need. AA, that's always on Monday. Tuesday's sex ed. Wednesday's anger management, Thursday's NA, Friday's parenting, and Sunday's worship service. Saturday we get a break."

"What's anger management?"

"Oh, we talk about what's makin' us angry, which is mostly each other. Seems like we get in as many fights in anger management as we do out here, once we start talkin' about bein' angry."

"You only talk about what happens in here? Not about anything on the outs?"

"Some about on the outs, but mostly about in here. Sure, there's plenty we're angry about on the outs, but, oh, girl, why start in on that? Nothin' goin' to change there."

She was right. Nothing going to change there.

The buzzer sounded again. "Come on. We got to put the vacuum away. Time for school."

Kate talked all morning about the Holy Roman Empire. Not everybody paid attention—what a surprise—but I did. It was interesting: the art and engineering and wars and literature. I especially loved the pictures of the mosaics, those odd, broken pieces of glass and stone making something so beautiful and complicated.

Dahlia returned from her room confinement at lunchtime, but she sat apart from everyone else and didn't speak to any of us. With her almost black lipstick and hair to match, she looked bizarre in pink slacks and a ruffled top. I figured that, for her,

47

wearing those clothes was a worse punishment than the room confinement.

In the afternoon we had to write about "My Best Friend." A month ago I would have written about Pam, but now I couldn't. I hadn't heard from her since the last time I called her from Juvie and she cut me short. Instead, I wrote about my bed. Right now, that was my best friend—a place I could go to forget about everything bad.

We played softball at P-E and Dahlia went to right field without any arguments when Connie told her to. She didn't speak to anyone for the whole game and she never even had to catch a ball. You hardly ever do in right field. Maybe Connie put her there on purpose, so she couldn't get her hands on a softball to throw at Shatasia's head. She struck out twice and popped out once and anybody with eyes could tell she wasn't really trying. So much for being excellent and superior at all times. No matter what she said, she just did it when she felt like it.

Damaris was catcher and she had a terrific arm for such a small person. Her eye wasn't as swollen as yesterday, but she still couldn't open it all the way. It didn't seem to interfere with her throwing aim.

Shatasia had taken one look at her and said, "You got yourself a bad one."

"He not so bad," Damaris said. "He just got a fast temper. Then he sorry."

"*You* the sorry one," Shatasia said. "What if you had a daughter and she come home lookin' like you do now? Would you think that was fine?"

"My mama gets beat up all the time," Damaris said. "She don't mind."

"Oh, no. I'm sure she just loves it. Huh," she said, walking away. "*You* the sorry one."

Damaris made a face at Shatasia's back.

Damaris and Toozdae had sat together at breakfast and had been whispering in class. They seemed two of a kind, both passive and sad-looking, though one was so dark and the other so fair. Maybe sorry people picked each other out.

Well, neither one of them would be picking me out. I was never going to be sorry.

After P-E, we cleaned up and went to sex ed. It was taught by a volunteer, a Hispanic woman named Soledad who had a table full of pamphlets, and, on the wall behind her, posters of male and female reproductive organs.

I remembered the sex-ed class we'd had at school. It was combined with a drug-education class, so we liked to say we were taking drugs and having sex. A lot of us really were, which made it even funnier.

I knew what all the stuff in the pictures was for. No mystery about how people had sex. What I wasn't always so sure about was why. It mostly started because some guy just kept bugging you until you gave in, and then he wouldn't wear a condom, so later you had to worry about getting a disease or ending up pregnant. The good part for me was after, when Ray would be so nice to me. Though sometimes he acted like he didn't even know me, which he could at *least* do because sex wasn't as good in real life as it was in the movies. Not with Ray, anyhow.

While we were finding seats, some of the girls started making remarks to Soledad.

"Oh, baby, baby. Yes, baby, yes. Yes!"

"Soledad, can we try out the birth-control stuff? Make sure it works?"

"Hey, Soledad, my homegirl got pregnant even though she put the condom on the banana like you showed us in class. You mean that's not where you're supposed to put it?"

"Hey, Soledad, let's talk about sex."

Soledad wore a red sweatshirt and jeans and had very big hair.

"Okay, okay," she said. "Settle down. I know this gets you all excited, but it's some serious stuff. You want to spend your whole life having babies? You know anybody like that? You want her life?"

"Hey, Soledad," one girl said. "Girls are supposed to have babies. Shatasia's got one. I want one."

"Okay, Shatasia," Soledad said. "You tell us. Was that baby part of your plans? I know you love her and she's adorable and brilliant and all, but was she part of a plan?"

Shatasia laughed. "You know I never had no plans. She was just something else that came along. And she's the *best* thing that ever just came along."

"So do you want three or four just like her? Or five or six?"

"Not me. Babies are different than what you think. Sharly, she's cute and all, but she's a lot of work. Nobody tells you that about babies, how much trouble they are, and how crazy so much cryin' can make you. Besides, I don't want no man now, either. One of those is *real* trouble."

"Well, let's talk about those men," Soledad said. "How many of you have had a man who was good to you, who thought about what you wanted and tried to help you get it even if it wasn't always so convenient for him to do that? Who said okay, fine, if you didn't feel like having sex or if you wanted him to wear a condom?" She waited. "Anybody?"

Lolly finally spoke. "They can be good to you sometimes."

"And sometimes is enough for you?" Soledad asked.

"It can be," she said. "When you're just so tired of people being mean to you or hurting you, and then somebody's nice to you even for a minute, it just feels good."

For the first time since I'd been at Girls' Rehab, there was complete silence. That rare kind of silence that meant everybody had heard Lolly. And not just heard her, but understood what she'd said.

Soledad spoke softly. "Wouldn't you rather have someone who was good to you all the time? There *are* guys like that."

Valencia made a frustrated sound. "Not where I'm from. All they want to do is two things, and they don't even try to hide it: they want to get you pregnant, and they want to get in fights until they die."

"Is that the kind of father you want for your babies, Valencia?" Soledad asked. "Somebody gone or dead?"

She shrugged. "If that's how it is. At least I'd have a baby. Somebody to love."

"Hey!" Soledad yelled. "Wake up, ladies! You can have better. I shouldn't have to be convincing you of this. You should know you deserve respect and kindness and love. It's not okay for people to treat you bad. There's something wrong with *them*, not with you."

"Oh, Soledad," Valencia said. "What planet are you coming from?"

"You girls," she said. "I'm just telling you there are guys out there who'll treat you right. You don't have to settle for the ones who won't. Remember that the next time some guy's knocking you around. I'm telling you, I know what I'm talking about. I had a guy who hit me, and who made me think it was my fault he had to do that. He had to break my jaw for me before I started looking for a guy who didn't think hitting was the way to solve problems."

"You could have hit him back," Sylviana said. She curled her strong, tattooed hands into fists.

"And then what happens, Sylviana?" Soledad asked, and answered her own question. "He hits you harder. And then maybe he'll say he's sorry, but he always does it again. That's a good time, right, Damaris?"

Damaris jumped as if she'd been pinched. "How you know my name? I never seen you before."

"The short answer is, it's part of my job to know who you are. The long answer is, every one of you is important to me. Every one of you is someone I want to see doing better."

Again the room was silent. Soledad's moment of kindness was so unexpected, so warmhearted, that it hushed us. It could be easier to know how to respond to abuse or neglect than to simple niceness, no strings attached.

Soledad went on. "That's why it's so important you learn how to take care of yourselves, be good to yourselves. That's why I'd like to see every one of you leave here with Norplant in your arms. No babies for at least five years. Give yourself a chance to get going."

"What if you don't know where to go?" Toozdae asked, in a voice as pale as her complexion. It made her seem about seven years old.

"How old are you, Toozdae?" Soledad asked. "Fourteen?"

Toozdae nodded.

"You're not *supposed* to know where you're going when you're fourteen. You're supposed to be staying in school and being a kid and doing things with your friends—things that don't include criminal activities. That's why you need five years without babies. That's how you figure out where you want to go."

Toozdae sighed and didn't say anything.

"*Ya con esto basta*," Soledad said. "That's enough of my lectures for today. But don't think that's the end of them. You'll be hearing more next time. Think about the Norplant." She held up a packet. "You see, it's just five little sticks. They go under the skin of your upper arm. It takes ten minutes, they're invisible, leave no scars, and you're safe from pregnancy. Come on up if you want a closer look. Just remember, you won't get pregnant, but you can still get a disease, including the big one. AIDS. What's the only way to avoid that?"

"Pack the plastic," several of the girls chanted in unison, and Soledad laughed.

"I guess you have been listening, after all. Next time we'll talk about how to get him to put it on."

Chairs screeched back and we went out the door, wandering back to the common room.

"Toozdae's fourteen?" I asked Shatasia.

"I guess. That's what she said."

"Why's she in here?"

"Prostitution."

"You're kidding."

Shatasia looked at me. "No, I'm not kiddin'. You don't know anybody who's done that?"

I shook my head.

"It's quick money. Good money, too, if you don't mind doin' the low-down sticky deed with a loony now and then. And there's a lot of old guys who get off on real young girls. I always looked too big and too tough for that. Nobody ever wanted to pay me for it, even though they didn't mind takin' it for free. But Toozdae's got a look, sort of like a Christmas tree angel, all that pale skin and blond hair. She made a lot of money."

Toozdae *did* look like an angel. That's why what Shatasia said surprised me so much.

"Girl, you been livin' in a cave?" Shatasia asked me. "Where you been, you don't know this stuff? Toozdae's mom's been on crack street and her father's long gone. She's got a bunch of little brothers and sisters who needed things they weren't getting from their mom. Toozdae was takin' care of everybody." Her voice lowered. "Includin' a stepbrother, I'm bettin'. If you know what I mean. He has a good job and she had to have his paycheck, too, to keep things together. So I'm guessin' she did what he wanted, even if she didn't like it."

"But I thought she was a prostitute. Why not do it with her stepbrother if she'll do it with anybody else?"

Shatasia gave me a scathing look. "Look here, girl. Business is one thing. You have what they want, they pay you for it, deal's done. Bein' blackmailed into it, or scared into it, or forced into it, that's something else. That's violence, even if it ain't *violent*, you know what I mean? Even prostitutes can get raped, right? I learned that from Soledad and she's right. Toozdae's stepbrother could make her do anything he wanted, long as he had that paycheck to threaten her with."

"Toozdae tells you all this?"

Shatasia lifted her shoulders. "No. Not one word. Even when I hint at it. But I watch him when he comes to visit. I see how Toozdae acts with him. I know what's going on."

"You could be wrong. He could just be a regular jerk."

"Could be," she said. "But I don't think so."

"Who's taking care of the brothers and sisters while she's in here? Not him, I hope."

"*I* don't know. I got my own stuff to think about. They're with the mom, I guess, or in placement, or somewhere."

"No wonder Toozdae always looks so sad."

"Huh. She should be celebratin'. She safe in here. And I hear her HIV test is negative. She *lucky*."

SEVEN

At dinner that night, the mood was up, excited. There was more talking than the night before, more laughing. Less tension.

"I'm gonna see my baby tonight, my Sharly," Shatasia crowed. "Y'all can see her, too, even if you can't squeeze her and sing to her like I can."

"I'll be having company tonight, too, maybe," Damaris said. "I'm thinking Revere'll be coming to see me." She smiled a beautiful slow smile. Now that her lower lip was less puffy, her mouth had a lush and generous look.

Shatasia leaned against me and whispered in my ear, "I wouldn't be countin' on that if I was her."

"No whispering, you two," called Malice. She patrolled the dining room while Barbara shuffled papers behind the desk at the other end of the room.

"Yeah," Sylviana said, chewing with her mouth open, her strong hands gripping her utensils. "You might be plotting an escape or a riot or something. Couple of dangerous characters, the two of you." She snorted, dismissing us. "In your dreams."

"Oh, shut up, Sylviana," Shatasia said. "You don't got to be pickin' a fight all the time. You don't got to be provin' all the time how down you are."

"I'm not proving nothing," Sylviana said. I saw that she had braced her muscular forearms on the table, ready to push herself upright. She cast a glance at Malice, who was occupied at another table, hassling Lolly and ruining what little dinner she managed to eat. "I'm down enough for somebody like you, you base bitch. You think you're so good now. You're just a base bitch, same as you ever were."

As if she was equipped with radar, Barbara, even far across the room, turned toward us at the sound of the word "bitch." "Everything all right over there?" she called. "I'm not hearing any improper language, am I? No one wants demerits, I'm sure." Malice looked over at us and then went back to her conversation.

"We're just fine, thank you," Sylviana replied innocently. Facing Shatasia, she smiled and spoke through her teeth. "You watch yourself, Shatasia. One day you might be getting too holy for the rest of us." She flung back her red-streaked hair.

"Oh, you shut your face, Sylviana," Shatasia said. "I got me a baby to take care of for the rest of her life. You think she wants a criminal for a mama? How do *you* like havin' one? I know what that feels like, too, and I don't want it for my baby girl."

The rest of us at the table had put our forks down and were watching the two of them warily.

"You don't tell me to shut up," Sylviana said. "My mom might be in prison, but she's a good mother. She loves me even if she's not good at showing it."

"Hard to show it when you're never around, not even mentionin' clean and sober, least never at the same time."

Sylviana stood up suddenly, her chair screeching back. Her

fists, with their tattoos across the knuckles, were clenched into knots.

Barbara stood up, too. From behind her desk, she said, "If you're finished, Sylviana, you can be excused. I'll come get those of you who'll have visitors."

Sylviana threw Barbara an evil look, then turned it on Shatasia and stalked out. Malice started for Shatasia, but Barbara said to her, "Everything's okay, Mary Alice. No problems."

Malice glared at Barbara, who ignored her and went back to her paperwork. Malice turned her glare back toward us.

Shatasia looked down at her hands, pressed flat onto the table, and took a deep breath. "That Sylviana, she is a *snake*," she said in a low voice. After another deep breath, she turned to me and said in a conversational voice, "You think you'll have a visitor tonight?"

Malice kept watching us.

"I doubt it," I said, but I was wondering if Ray would come. I knew he couldn't have gotten my letter yet, but I needed to see him, and I hoped that somehow he would feel my need and respond to it.

"My grandma, she's always the first one here," Shatasia said.

"All right," Malice said. "Dinner's over. Start cleaning up. Get your useless butts moving."

We were doing homework in the common room when Shatasia's grandmother was the first visitor to be announced, on the stroke of seven-thirty. Visiting took place in the dining room, so I knew I wouldn't be seeing Sharly. I was surprised how disappointed I felt about that.

I was wondering if I wanted to start reading *The Member of the Wedding* when Barbara came to me and said, "You have a visitor, Dallas."

"I do?" I asked. "A male one?"

"Good guess," she said. "Must be the answer to a prayer."

"As long as it's not my father."

"It's not," Barbara said. "Too young for that. You want to do any primping first?"

"No." It could only be Ray, and whatever was going on between me and him wasn't going to be helped by whether or not I brushed my hair, I knew that.

He looked different after less than a month. His thick dark hair was longer. And he looked bigger somehow, more formidable.

"Hi," I said, keeping my expression neutral, leaving it to him to let me know what his mood was. "I wrote you."

"Yeah?" He stood, his hands in the back pockets of his jeans. "I didn't get it."

"I just mailed it today. I wanted you to know where I was."

"I heard. The grapevine."

"Pretty good. I just got here yesterday. Sit down." I sat across the table from him. Close enough for him to touch me if he wanted to, but not so close that he'd feel like he had to. I was always doing those calculations with him, wondering how much I could expect from him, how much he'd be willing to give me, how much I could push before he turned away from me.

"So," he said. "How are you doing?" He looked around. "This seems like an okay place."

I shrugged. "It's all right. If you like being locked up. It's better than Juvie."

"Yeah. That place is a pit. Both times I was there, it was too crowded and too noisy. And the food—pure garbage."

"Food's okay here."

"That's good." He twisted around in his chair so that he was facing to the side, away from me.

"I thought you'd write to me while I was there."

Without looking at me, he said, "Yeah, well, you know me. Not so good with the written word."

Or the spoken one, I thought. "Well, I'm glad you came tonight."

"Yeah."

I wasn't going to ask him why he'd come. He'd tell me or he wouldn't, no matter what I said.

Behind Ray, at another table, Shatasia sat with Sharly on her lap. Shatasia's grandmother sat opposite her with three other kids, who looked to be between four and seven. They were coloring and arguing about who got to have the red crayon. Shatasia's grandmother was thin, with a thinness that looked strong, like a bowstring. She put her hand on one child's head and leaned down to whisper in another's ear. With a grudging look, he loosened his hold on the red crayon, gave it to her, and took a green one from the box. Shatasia lifted Sharly's little hand and waved it at me. Sharly grinned as a bead of drool slid from her bottom lip onto her overalls.

I gazed across the room, where Sylviana sat with someone who could only be her sister, they looked so much alike. The sister wore her hair the same way, with the same red streak, and her black leather skirt, what there was of it, was so tight she had to sit on the edge of her chair. She chewed gum viciously and kept looking in a purse mirror to touch up her dark purple lipstick. Sylviana leaned toward her, talking low and fast.

"Have you seen Pam?" I asked.

This time he looked at me and then away again. "Pam? Sure. She's around. Why?"

"I just wondered. She hasn't written either."

"She said she talked to you on the phone."

"I wouldn't call it much of a conversation. She was always getting ready to go somewhere. What's going on with her?"

"She didn't tell you she and Sonny broke up?"

"No. Not a word. What happened?"

He shot me another quick look. "Sonny thought she was interested in somebody else."

"And was she?"

"Yeah." He gave a low laugh. "Turns out she was."

I was beginning to get the picture. But I couldn't imagine he'd come here to rub my nose in it. What did he want?

He leaned forward on his elbows, finally facing me. "We wanted to say thanks. For, you know, not saying we were with you at the Jiffy-Spot. That was a straight-up thing you did. Took guts. Even if you weren't thinking about what would happen to you if you *did* tell."

At last I got it. He was kissing me off. With a compliment, to ease what little conscience he had. And a threat, in case the compliment didn't work.

"So you're with her now, right?" I asked.

"With who?" he asked, trying to look puzzled. "Pam, you mean?"

"Don't treat me like I'm stupid," I said. "I know." There was no point in worrying about annoying him now. Whether I annoyed him or not wasn't going to make any difference. He was gone. He and Pam had burned my last bridge out from under me while I hung on to it.

His expression was hard and tight. "How? Who told you?"

I stood. "A little bird. Don't worry about it." I turned away from him.

As I started across the room, I heard him say, "Bye, Dallas. Be good."

I stumbled over a chair leg just before I reached the door. A guy about nineteen, good-looking, with black hair and heavy-lidded dark eyes, rose from where he was sitting at a table with Toozdae and a tired-looking woman whose dark roots were showing. He took my arm. "You okay?" he asked.

His hand moved on my upper arm, his knuckles pressing into the side of my breast. I pulled my arm away. "I'm fine," I said. As I went through the door, I heard Toozdae say, in her pale voice, "You're not supposed to talk to anybody but me, Mark. It's the rules, and I'm the one that gets the demerits."

He laughed. "Since when are you so crazy about rules?"

The door swung shut behind me and I stood in the hallway, pinching the bridge of my nose and looking up. After a moment, I went back to the common room to be searched and to finish my homework.

Just after nine, Shatasia came to our room, beaming. "Now tell me my Sharly's the cutest baby you ever saw."

"Sharly's the cutest baby I ever saw," I said dutifully, looking up from *The Member of the Wedding*. I was trying to read, but my mind was so full of what Ray had told me, and of what it meant, that I couldn't remember a word I'd read. How could I ever have thought Pam was my friend?

"Well, I *know* it," Shatasia said. "Oh, I hate sayin' goodbye to her."

"Who were the other kids?"

"One's my little brother, and the other two are my cousins."

"They all live with your grandmother?"

"Yeah." She was undressing. "There's a few other grandkids that come when things are bad at home, with the fightin' and drinkin' and all, and then they go back." She put on her robe.

"Will you live with your grandmother, too, when you get out?"

"I don't know if I can. I might have to go to a group home or something like that for a while first. Some judges like to make it hard for you to get back to the place where you got in trouble to start with. I guess they think the longer you're away from it, the more you lose interest."

"Have you?"

She lifted her shoulders. "I don't want to get back in trouble, I know that. But when it's all around you, well, you know. And I have to say it," she added. "Livin' straight sometimes sounds almighty dull. I can't say I always mind the knucklin' up out there. It can be such a freeze, you know?"

"I do know," I said. "There's nothing like it to get your adrenaline going."

"I just don't think it's the best thing for babies."

"What about Sharly's dad? Will he help you?"

"Hah!" she said harshly. "He helped himself *to* me, that's about it. And yeah, I was kinda sprung on him, I admit it. But he's not gonna be there for me anymore. Or for Sharly. She's mine. Hey, I got to go shower now."

When she returned, she got in bed, arranging her pillow and her stuffed rabbit in some precise way. We were quiet for a while.

"Don't we get a bedtime story tonight?" I finally asked.

"Not on Tuesday or Sunday. I guess it's too much on top of

visitors. Seems like at least some music would be good, though. Everybody's kind of jumped up on those nights. You can read," she said. "I just want to lie here and think about my Sharly."

I picked up the book and began reading again about Frankie Addams, who "belonged to no club and was a member of nothing in the world. Frankie had become an unjoined person who hung around in doorways, and she was afraid."

EIGHT

At breakfast, Sylviana said to Toozdae, "I saw your brother visiting you again last night. He's so hot."

"He's my stepbrother," Toozdae mumbled, her head bent over her oatmeal. "I've told you that before."

"Oh, yeah," Sylviana said. "Was that your mom? I haven't seen her before."

"It's the first time she's come," Toozdae said softly. "She's been in rehab. She's home now. And she says she's fine and she's going to get a job and everything will be okay."

"He lives with her?" Sylviana asked. Toozdae nodded. "I don't think I'd trust him with her. He's got those eyes, you know what I mean? I like those kind of eyes. They're, you know, dangerous eyes. Sexy eyes. I bet your stepdad keeps an eye on those two."

"My stepdad's gone," Toozdae said.

"You mean that hunk-o-matic is alone with your mom? Then I can guess what's going on there. Don't tell me you haven't had a taste of him, too. I would if he was in my house."

Toozdae's face grew paler, if that was possible, and a red blemish on her cheek stood out like a headlight. "You don't know anything, Sylviana," she said.

"Hey!" Sylviana said, coming half out of her chair, her tattooed hands flat on the table. "You dissing me?"

Toozdae concentrated on her oatmeal. Damaris, sitting next to Toozdae, looked nervously back and forth between Toozdae and Sylviana.

"You hear me, bitch?" Sylviana asked.

Connie came up behind Sylviana and put her hands on her shoulders, pressing her down into her chair. "Take it easy," she said. "Did I hear a certain word you're not supposed to say in here?"

"I didn't hear nothing," Sylviana said. She looked around the table. "Any of you *witches* hear anything?"

No one spoke.

Connie squeezed Sylviana's shoulders. "I must be getting hard of hearing."

"No you aren't," Dahlia said from the foot of the table.

Connie pressed harder on Sylviana, who was trying to stand. "I'm not?"

"No. She said what you thought she said."

Dahlia had balls, no doubt about it. I would bet Sylviana wasn't going to let that go by.

"Are you sure?" Connie asked.

Dahlia nodded. "I'm sure."

"Anybody else care to verify that?" Connie asked.

Nobody did. Toozdae concentrated on her oatmeal. Damaris and Shatasia stared at the wall, Valencia chewed on a fingernail, and I just blanked over the same way I did when my father talked to me.

Connie spoke. "Well, Dahlia's word will have to be good enough, since it agrees with what I heard. You know what that means, Sylviana. Twenty-four hours' room confinement. Demerits don't seem to work with you. You know there's to be no bad language in here, nothing inflammatory, and still you keep at it. You're supposed to be learning to control yourself. You call someone a bitch or worse on the outs and you're likely to get hurt. I won't let that happen here."

Sylviana stood. "You're in outer space, Connie, if you think I can walk away from somebody dissing me on the outs."

"Then you better get used to being behind bars because that's where you'll spend a lot of time if you don't figure out a way to do things differently than the way you've done them so far."

"The way I've done them so far works fine," Sylviana said, and walked away toward the door to the bedrooms, with Connie behind her.

Valencia turned to Dahlia. "I bet you're going to be sorry you did that," she said.

"I don't think so," Dahlia said. "Maybe the best place for her *is* behind bars. She's an insult to Aryan society."

"I don't know what that means, Aryan society," Valencia said. "But I don't think she's any more of an insult to it than you are."

"Okay," Connie said, returning. "That's enough. If you need to express yourselves, maybe Kate can assign you a subject to write about. Now get going with your jobs before school starts."

As Valencia and I cleared the breakfast dishes, Valencia said, "That Dahlia, she stupid or nuts or what, with all that Aryan crap?" She shook her head. "You know, Sylviana's in here for almost killing a girl with a knife. One of our own homegirls, too, not even somebody in another gang. I've known her all my life and she even says we're friends, but I'm still scared of her, and Dahlia should be, too. When she gets her mind on something, nothing stops her. She told me last night after dinner Malice came to her room and called her some names, ones *we* can't use here, like whore and spic, and Malice said Sylviana didn't deserve anything good to happen to her. Ever. Sylviana says Malice should be watching her back now."

"We probably all should be," I said. "Sylviana seems like she's mad at everybody."

"You're right. But more at Malice lately than anybody. She thinks Malice is on the wrong side of the locked door."

Connie must have talked to Kate about expressing ourselves because the topic for writing that day was "What Makes Me Feel Insulted and What I Do About It." Between my father, Ray, and Pam, being insulted was a subject I had had plenty of recent experience with, but I still couldn't think of anything to do about it that made me feel any better.

Group that afternoon was anger management. It was led by a guy named Nolan. He wore jeans, Reeboks, and an Arizona Wildcats T-shirt. He tried to cover up his baby face with a beard, but you could still tell it was there. He had good eyes: cocoa brown and smart, with long lashes that made him look sweet and dim, like a camel or something.

"Hi, ladies," Nolan said. "What's poppin'?"

Nobody spoke.

"Oh, it's like that?" he said. "Who is it this time? Sylviana again?"

Toozdae was the one who finally nodded. "She never stops.

She bugs me about stuff at home. She says things about my mother and my stepbrother. She picks on everybody. How can we make her stop?"

"You know you can't make her do anything," he said. "All you can do is take care of yourselves: leave the scene, go to Connie or Kate or Barbara or *anybody*. Don't respond to her."

Toozdae shook her head. "It doesn't work. She follows you if you try to leave, or waits for you if you go to Connie, or keeps at you until you *have* to say something. Why can't you make her stop?"

"Well, room confinement does that for a little while, but she'll have to be the one to decide to stop for good. You should know by now you can't change anybody but yourself. And if she won't stop, she'll have to be the one to take what comes next. It won't always be something she likes."

"She's never going to change," Valencia said. "She's been the same her whole life. Except on the outs sometimes she's funny and does nice things for you. In here, she's mad all the time. But, in or out, she's unpredictable and she's scary."

"Well, it's not an accident she's that way," Nolan said. "Something's made her so angry and self-protective. Just the way things have made us all the way we are. But don't forget, the same experiences can make two people act completely differently. Some people respond to hard things by fighting back. Some by getting tougher and smarter. And some by giving up. You get to choose."

"It's not choosing," Lolly said, her pointed chin resting in her palm, propped by her spindly arm. "You just are the way you are."

"Oh, no," Nolan said. "There's plenty of room for choice.

69

But the problem is that choosing is hard. We hate things that are hard. And how much you want to change can depend on what kind of rewards you get for being how you are. Let's say every time you try to be tough, or smart, somebody smacks you in the face. That might make you stop trying to be tough. Or smart. Or you may learn how to smack back. Or you may endure the smacks if you think it'll get you what you want. It's very complicated, the way we all behave."

We were quiet, chewing this over. I was surprised to hear people weren't programmed at the factory to be who they were. I didn't know if I believed Nolan about making choices of how to be. Oh, maybe I should have chosen not to rob the Jiffy-Spot. Yeah, that would have been smart. But at the time I'd felt like it was something I had to do, as if there was no choice. Could I have chosen not to be friends with Pam and Ray and Sonny? It didn't feel that way. Could I have chosen to be the daughter my father wanted? Definitely not possible.

"Okay," Nolan said. "Anybody else want to say what's making them angry?"

"Graduate students who think they know what they're doing but really don't have a clue," Dahlia said.

"Do you mean me?" Nolan asked.

"Do you qualify?" Dahlia answered.

Nolan looked at her with his beautiful quiet eyes. "What makes you think I'm a graduate student?"

"Aren't you?"

"Do you think there's something wrong with being a graduate student?" he asked.

It seemed as if all they were going to do was go back and forth asking each other questions, with neither of them answering any.

70

"Only with the ones who don't know what they're doing. What do you think we are, babies? You think we're going to hear you say we should be what you want us to be and that'll make it happen? We're already tougher than you want to know about. And smarter, too. You wouldn't last five minutes in some of the places we go. Remember, we're felons. The real thing."

"You seem very angry," Nolan said.

Dahlia laughed, shook her head, and slumped back in her chair, her arms crossed on her chest.

"Would anybody else like to volunteer anything?" Nolan asked. "As long as we're talking about anger?"

Glances slid to Dahlia and then back to Nolan. No one spoke.

"You may never have noticed this," Nolan said, "but one person can sometimes set the tone for a whole group. Even if some in the group have other ideas. Maybe you've seen this in the gangs you've belonged to. How one person can frighten or bully the others. Or inspire and encourage the others. Think of that. Inspiration and courage. What a concept." He waited, but no one spoke. "It's hard to go against a strong leader, even when you know she's wrong. Or he, naturally. Look at the power Adolf Hitler had. We know there were some Nazis who didn't agree with him, but most of them kept very quiet. They were afraid, of course, but so were the others, the ones who spoke up, who resisted. How do you suppose they were different?" He paused, but we were quiet. "What do you think it would feel like, to do what you thought was right, even if no one else agreed with you, even if you were afraid? Any ideas?"

Nope. Not a one.

After he listened to us be silent some more, Nolan took a long breath and said, "Okay. Well, go out there and don't let your anger manage you." He sounded tired.

As we left, Damaris whispered to me, "Who's that Hitler person Nolan said? And those Nazis? That some gang I should know?"

NINE

On the outs, I was like Frankie in *The Member of the Wedding*—
not a belonger. Except with Pam and then later with Ray and
Sonny, too. I spent a lot of time alone in my room, avoiding my
father, and I hadn't exactly been Miss Congeniality at school, either. I wasn't used to being part of a big group doing everything
together the way I had to be at GRC, where there was no such
thing as privacy.

Meals together and exercise together; classes together and
jobs together; groups and TV time, always shared. Even showers, alone behind a thin curtain, were still communal, since others were always showering at the same time, in their own
cubicles, and I could hear them splashing and dropping things.

When you had no choice but to be with others all the time,
craving solitude was asking for trouble, and I had been sure I'd
be a candidate for it.

My big surprise was that I usually didn't mind all the company, the commotion, the crowding. In the pack of girls, I didn't
feel as invisible as I had on the outs, and if it took a group of
felons to accomplish that, it was good enough for me.

.   .   .

One unseasonably hot afternoon when we'd been playing basketball, Kate, Connie, and Malice, who had traded that day's
night shift for someone else's day shift, had given us a break to
sprawl in the shade panting and drinking cup after cup of
Gatorade from the cooler.

"You think Malice has a date tonight and that's why she
traded shifts?" Shatasia asked. "What kind of guy you think is
Malice's type?"

"One that's deaf, dumb, and blind," one of the other girls
said.

"Oh, man," Sylviana said, "would I ever like a nice cold beer."

Many voices groaned and agreed. "A couple of 40s would really be good."

"You ever have a Blue Lagoon?" Sylviana asked. "Oooh,
they're good."

"What's in them?" someone asked.

"I don't know, but they're blue. My homegirl ChaCha, she
floats a coffee bean in hers, or a chocolate M&M, and she calls
it a Toilet Bowl."

"Typical," Dahlia said.

"You ever have Sex on the Beach?" Susan, a new girl, asked
Sylviana, distracting her before she could react to Dahlia.

"Yeah," Sylviana said, "but I don't like it. It hurts and you get
sand all up you and in your hair."

"Not that," Susan said, laughing. "I mean the drink. It's called
Sex on the Beach. It's clear, no color, and man, it hits you like a
hammer. Only time I had them, I got tore up from the floor up.
I woke up in some strange place with some strange dude. I
never will have one of those again. But it went down good."

"Probably didn't come up so good," Sylviana said.

"You got that right," Susan said. Susan was built hard and

square, with no waistline and the most tattoos of anybody in GRC—some homemade gang designs and some elaborate professional jobs. But she seemed a lot younger than she actually was, as if she wasn't quite all there. Maybe too many Sex on the Beaches had killed off some brain cells.

"Nothing gets you as sprung out as speed-fry," Damaris said. "I did some hard trippin' with that. Saw whole villages on my arms, with animals dancin', and my arm hairs wavin' like trees." She shook her head, remembering.

I flicked a look at Kate, Connie, and Malice, across the basketball court, heads together. We knew we weren't supposed to be talking about sex or drugs or alcohol or our crimes or gangs or anything our lives were really about except in one of the groups where some grownup could make us quit whenever things got really interesting. Talking about these things to each other was supposed to make us want to do them. To tell the truth, I couldn't tell the difference between talking about them in group and talking about them on the basketball court. The stories were the same.

Then I shrugged mentally. What did I care? I liked to listen to the stories the others told. I didn't say much myself, but I understood that you could learn a lot by listening. You could even learn something you might be able to use against the person who said it. Silence was a weapon neither Sylviana nor Dahlia, with their big motor-mouths, always ready to front someone off, could understand.

Besides, I didn't have much to add to the conversation. I'd smoked enough pot, and drunk plenty of beer, but that was milk and cookies compared to what some of the others had done. I'd dropped acid once and taken Ecstasy at a party, but I'd avoided anything else. I was afraid of getting really addicted, of losing my self and my strength to booze or drugs. Too, I didn't want to have to take up full-time robbery to pay for whatever I got addicted to. And I didn't want to die. Listening to the others tell their stories of horse tranquilizers, sherm sticks, monkey juice, primos, four-day drug-induced comas, non-stop sex with strangers, and hallucinations of being chased by cars, I thanked whatever self-preservation instinct had prevented me from having the same stories.

"Anybody ever try Body-Bag?" someone asked.

"Body-Bag? Never heard of it. You givin' me a drag line?"

"No, no, it's real. Heroin wrapped in a piece of balloon, don't ask me why. I never had any. I heard a body bag is what you go home in if you use it. I ain't *that* stupid."

"I love that glass pipe. Oooh, it makes you feel good."

I thought about degrees of stupidity, including my own. What was the difference between being stupid enough for the Chronic, or crack, or crystal, but not for Body-Bag? It was all the same.

It was actually remarkable that my fellow bad girls had been able to commit any crimes at all, considering how stoned they were most of the time. Some of them couldn't even remember their first few days at Juvie, because they'd been sobering up or coming down off some high.

The more we talked, the more excited everybody got, trying to top each other's stories, max each other, be the most down. Finally, our noise level reached Kate and Connie and Malice, who looked sharply at us with her snaky eyes. Without a word, the three of them crossed the basketball court at just under a run.

"Too hot out here," Connie said. "Let's go in and cool off."

Kate added, "It got quiet all of a sudden over here. We weren't talking about anything we shouldn't be, were we?"

"Who, us?" Sylviana asked. "Why, you know us better than that, don't you?"

Malice gave her a hard, undeceived look. "I know you as well as anybody ever will," she said. "So don't try to fool me about anything."

"Oooh, I'm an open book," Sylviana said. Her eyes narrowed. "But I'm written in a language you can't read."

"I wouldn't be counting on that," Malice said.

"Count on it," Sylviana said, and we went inside.

Malice watched herself when Connie or Barbara or Kate were around, but when she was alone she pushed us and called us ugly names: nigger and beaner and slut. She told Damaris and Lolly and Toozdae that they were worthless, that they were doomed on the outs and even inside, that they were too dumb to learn enough to do themselves any good. Toozdae took it with a closed face and a faraway look, but Damaris recoiled in fear and sank into herself, terrified of her own dismal future. And Lolly went straight to the bathroom to lose whatever meal she'd most recently eaten.

Malice called me Queen of Denial because she thought I considered myself too good to be inside. She said Shatasia had better teach Sharly to be a better felon than her mother was. She said none of us would ever have legal jobs or friends or nice things unless they were stolen.

And what she said to the rest of us was nothing to the way she treated Dahlia and Sylviana. She called Dahlia the Dyke.

"That bitch," Dahlia said to Shatasia and me. "That *bitch*.

She knows how I hate anything like that. Men and women together are the only natural combination. Anything else is perversion. What makes her think she can call me that? She might as well call me what she calls Sylviana—it's as big an insult. But with Sylviana it's true."

Malice called Sylviana the Spic Whore all the time now. She never used her name unless one of the other p.o.'s was in earshot. She loved to see Sylviana so enraged and so powerless.

"She says stuff like that to everybody," Shatasia told Dahlia. "Means nothing except she's got a bad attitude and a bad mouth."

"It's not acceptable," Dahlia said. "She also treats Sylviana and me differently than she does the rest of you, and she's so slick the other p.o.'s don't know what's going on. We've got the only single rooms. She comes in at night and shines her flashlight in our faces to wake us up and then she says she's just checking on us. She makes us shower in cold water. With my mental strength it's easy for me to do that, but I don't like how she tells us we have to because we're too hot for our own good. She gives us trouble at dinner so we don't get to eat until our food's cold. She picks out the worst clothes for us from Friends of Felons, so we go around here looking like freaks. I understand why she's after Sylviana, but what have I done to her? I have nothing in common with Sylviana. *Nothing.*"

"You can't figure her out," I said. "She doesn't think like a normal person." And neither do you, I could have added, but didn't. And that's what she had in common with Sylviana.

We thought about taking our complaints about Malice to the grievance committee, but those who had been there the longest said it was no use.

"The p.o.'s always win," they said. "We're the criminals, remember? Who'd believe us? And then things just get worse because Malice'll find out and be pissed. Think about Malice when she's *really* pissed, not just regular pissed, the way she usually is." So we didn't try to do anything official. None of us trusted any official bodies, anyway. Such groups never saw things the same way we did.

But there were unofficial ways to solve problems. We began to develop elaborate scenarios for Malice—car wrecks and radios falling into her bathwater, fatal food poisoning and rabid dog bites, falls from balconies and down elevator shafts.

"I wish Malice would just have a heart attack and drop dead," Damaris said one afternoon during free time when several of us were slumped on the couches in front of the TV.

"She's going to need some help," Dahlia said. Her voice was calm and deliberate.

"What?" Damaris asked. She and Toozdae and I turned away from the TV to look at Dahlia. There was something different in her tone, something that alerted all of us.

"She's going to need some help," Dahlia enunciated. "At dropping dead."

"Where's that help comin' from?" Damaris asked cautiously.

"Care to make a guess?" Dahlia asked.

Damaris shook her head. "Nope."

She and Toozdae turned back to the TV blank-faced, as if they'd slammed a door between themselves and Dahlia.

I stared at Dahlia, who was painting her fingernails that deep, almost black burgundy she loved. She couldn't mean what that sounded like, could she? Not like one of our Malice fantasies, but like serious planning.

TEN

Two nights later, Valencia, Dahlia, Sylviana, and I were the last to shower, while Malice stood outside the stalls, shouting at us over the sound of the water. Barbara was supervising the other girls in the locker room as they dried off and got ready for bed.

"Scrub good, you little sluts," Malice said to us. "See if you can wash off the stink you came in here with. See if you can ever be clean again."

What is her problem, I wondered. How did she get to be such a big-mouthed monster?

"You're not trying to turn on any hot water, are you, Dyke? Are you, Spic Whore?"

Then I heard the slap of wet feet on tile, a shout, a gurgling sound, and a lot of scuffling. I stood still under the hot water, listening. The scuffling sounds went on. Did I really want to know what was happening?

I could hear voices, too, but because of the noise of the showers I couldn't make out what they were saying.

"Dallas?" Valencia said cautiously from the shower next to me. "Are you okay?"

"Yeah," I said. "How about you?"

"Yeah."

We were silent again, and the whispering and scuffling went on, punctuated by thuds and cracks of something against the tile.

I stepped out of the shower and wound my towel around me, leaving the water running. I stuck my head out of the cubicle, looking first in Valencia's direction, where I saw nothing, then in the other, where I saw Malice's feet sticking out of Dahlia's shower cubicle, kicking and struggling for leverage. There were puddles on the floor and the legs of Malice's pants were wet. The voices I heard were Dahlia's and Sylviana's.

I turned into Valencia's cubicle and pulled the curtain back an inch. "Dahlia and Sylviana have got Malice."

Valencia stared, her arms wrapped protectively around her centerfold body. "Oh, my God. What are you going to do?"

Me? I thought. Why should *I* do anything? Whatever Dahlia and Sylviana were going to do, they'd already done. Did I care what happened to Malice?

"I don't know," I said and closed the curtain. Then I turned the other way, toward Malice and Sylviana and Dahlia.

Malice was on the ground, with Dahlia and Sylviana crouched over her, the two of them naked and dripping. Sylviana was holding Malice down inside the shower. Dahlia's fingers were tangled in the tight curls of Malice's perm and she rhythmically yanked her head up and cracked it down on the shower floor. Malice appeared to be unconscious and there was a stream of red running from her head, mixing with the cold shower water and going down the drain.

Dahlia and Sylviana looked up at me, their eyes glazed and brutal.

"Want to help?" Sylviana asked.

I was frozen with fascination and horror at their casual cruelty. I shook my head. "You're going to kill her," I said.

"So?" Dahlia said. "She's earned it." Then she cracked Malice's head once again onto the tile.

I backed away from them, then turned and ran for Barbara.

Dahlia and Sylviana were sent back to Juvie that same night and it was a done deal that they'd be going to a work camp as soon as there was a trial. They might even be tried as adults, and then it would be worse: real prison.

Malice had a fractured skull, broken ribs, and a lot of cuts and bruises, but she wasn't going to die. Whether she'd be looking for a new line of work was another question. So was whether her brain would ever be good enough for *Jeopardy* again.

Some of the girls were mad at me that I hadn't let Dahlia and Sylviana finish the job. At the same time, they were celebrating that Malice was gone. We all were.

If we were celebrating, the coaches were not. They were stern and quiet and watched us more closely than ever. There was no kidding around with them, no looseness. They were shocked, as we all were, and they were afraid. In the daily routines, it was easy to forget that some of us were capable of anything at any time. Even murder.

At lunch, Toozdae said, "I know it sounds funny, but I always felt safe in here. My . . . my work was dangerous and being at home wasn't much better. Here, the coaches look out for you. And there's good food and bedtime stories, and it should be safe."

"I don't feel safe nowhere," Valencia said. "Nobody cares

enough to look out for you all the time. And there'll always be somebody like Sylviana waiting to go off."

"But I thought the coaches could keep that from happening," Toozdae said. "I thought the rules would work."

It made me sad that her illusion of safety had been broken. I was only two years older than she was, and I hadn't had the rough experiences she had, but I still felt that she was a baby who only wanted protection and affection. And who wasn't getting much of either.

"Don't y'all think it's strange," Damaris asked, "how Sylviana and Dahlia did it together when they hated each other so much?"

"Maybe they hated Malice more," I said. "Maybe they didn't plan it together, but just jumped when the chance came."

"Whatever," Shatasia said. "They's where they should have been in the first place. You *can* feel safe in here, Toozdae."

Apparently, Shatasia had the same impulse I did to comfort Toozdae.

"People like them's too dangerous to be in with us," she went on. "We got a chance. They aren't changin' their ways."

"You think we got a chance?" Damaris asked, her great dark eyes worried. "Malice didn't think so."

"You ever wonder why somebody'd want a job working in a place like this?" Shatasia asked, mixing peas into her mashed potatoes. "I think it's three reasons. One, they hate us and want a chance to be over us. Two, they love us and want to help us."

Valencia snickered at this and said, "Oh, right."

Shatasia gave her a look and went on. "Three, they were like us and they feel comfortable with us. I'll bet my booty Kate's number two and Connie's number three."

"And Malice was number one?" I asked.

"What do you think?" Shatasia asked. "Or maybe she was number three *and* number one. But she was number one for sure." She turned back to Damaris. "So, yeah, I think we got a chance. Somebody like Malice is not going to be the person who tells me my future. Why you so ready to believe what somebody else thinks? Why you don't make up your own future?"

"Cause I don't know how," Damaris said, and her voluptuous lower lip trembled.

"You think I knew how?" Shatasia asked. "You think I sat down and said, Shatasia M'Tafi Jefferson, the best way to have a good life is to join a gang, carry a gun, and get pregnant when you're fourteen?"

Damaris giggled. "So why did you?"

"Why you think? Because nobody told me nothin' else. I never *thought*. I just *did*. Well, in here, you can learn how to think about a future. Maybe you don't care as much as me cause I got Sharly. But it's here, what you want. Kate's good at it. So's Nolan. And usin' that ole Norplant like Soledad says is somethin' I'm goin' to be doin'."

"You think I've got a chance, too?" Toozdae asked.

"Course you do. But one thing you got to do is start takin' care of yourself. You know what I mean. You're not the mama to those little kids. You're a kid, too. Let your mom start doing for them. She's clean now, right?"

"Yes. She's got a job and she's going to her meetings. She says she's going to make it this time. I hope so," she said quietly, "because I'll be getting out soon."

"Then you got your chance. You can go to school and stay straight and not have to do any of that stuff like before." Shatasia could sound so cold and stern, as if she had all the answers and nobody else even had the right questions.

"It's hard."

"And what got you in here wasn't hard?" Shatasia asked.

"Yeah. But it's easy in a way, too."

"Easy cause you just let it happen. Hard's when you fight."

"I don't know if I can," Toozdae said. "I don't know if I can grow that kind of strength. Why can't I stay here where it's safe?"

Alone in the bathroom in the few minutes before class started after lunch, I stood looking at myself in the mirror over the sink. I was surprised to see that I looked the same as I always had. You'd think so many changes would show on the outside—getting arrested, being deserted by my father and dumped by my boyfriend; watching Malice get beaten almost to death—but I looked untouched. Maybe even blander than I used to, as if some experiences had been erased rather than added.

I heard a sound and realized I wasn't alone. Under the door of one of the stalls I could see the bottoms of someone's shoes, someone who was kneeling on the floor in front of the toilet.

"Lolly?" I said.

"Who's that?"

"It's Dallas. Is that you, Lolly?"

The feet stood up. "Yeah, it's me."

"Are you okay?"

The stall door opened and Lolly came out, wiping the back of her hand across her mouth. "I've got a nervous stomach," she explained. "That thing with Malice has got me all upset." She rinsed out her mouth and spat in the sink.

"It's got everybody upset."

"I've seen a lot, you know," Lolly said. "My sister, she got whacked in a drive-by, and my old boyfriend, he's in a wheelchair now, and I got me a few knife scars, too. But it's not something I ever got used to. Not like some. You know, they think, well, if it's my time it's my time and that's it. But me, I'm walking around nervous a lot, you know. It's hard on my stomach. Hard to digest, or something."

"I wondered," I said. "You're so thin."

"Yeah. Lot of people, they think I got one of those eating things, you know. Disorders. I guess I do, but not the way they think. I wish I *didn't* keep getting sick. I was thinking in here I could maybe feel safer, relax a little, but that's not happening. I don't feel that safe, or that relaxed."

"Yeah," I said. "I can see you need some serious stress control. Maybe you could start biting your nails or cracking your knuckles or doing yoga instead of unswallowing."

Lolly grinned. "I already bite my nails. I tried the knuckles but I can't do it. Maybe it's just a guy thing. And I don't know nothing about yoga. Got any other ideas?"

"No. How about school?"

"Man, *that* won't work. I'm no good at it. It just upsets me more."

"I meant, maybe we ought to go. It's time for class."

Lolly giggled. "Oh. Okay. I don't want demerits for being late."

"That'd be something else to stress about, right?"

"Life's a bitch, isn't it?" Lolly asked, holding open the bathroom door.

I was back in the bathroom after dinner with Shatasia, both of us on our knees, scrubbing toilets.

"I'll say this for getting money the illegal way," Shatasia said. "It's quicker than doing this, and it gives you that nice kind of kick you don't get from this."

"Yeah," I said. "This makes selling drugs seem like a good career move."

"Until you get caught," Shatasia said. "Far as I know, there ain't no penalty for cleaning bathrooms."

"You think you'll always get caught?" I asked. "Or can you be so good you never do?"

"Oh, there's probably a few so good or so lucky they don't get caught. But it's not anybody I know. And it's not goin' to be me. I been caught too many times already to think that."

"You have?"

"I got caught and let go eleven times before I finally got run in. I was startin' to think I could keep goin' that way, but now I know different. Cops'll give you a break at first if you're a girl, but once you've been inside, no more breaks."

I sat back on my heels, holding my scrub brush, and thought about that. No more breaks. I hadn't even gotten the one the judge was willing to give me, because of my father. I shook my head, moved to another toilet, and started scrubbing again.

"How come," Shatasia asked, "you didn't just let Dahlia and Sylviana go on Malice? How come you called Barbara?"

I stopped scrubbing. "I don't know. I've thought about it and I can't even remember deciding whether to help or not. It was just . . . automatic."

Shatasia stopped scrubbing too, and wiped her forehead with her sleeve. "I guess maybe you got a workin' conscience. That's something Nolan likes to talk about, a workin' conscience. It's knowing what's the right thing, and doing it even when you don't want to. You know, there's people don't know what in the hell he's talkin' about."

"Do you?"

"Hey!" Shatasia sounded insulted. "How I'm goin' to bring Sharly along if I don't know that? I know I've done bad things. Lots of them. But I always knew when I was doin' something I shouldn't be. I just didn't care. That's different."

I wasn't sure how it was different, even while I understood what she meant. What use was a working conscience if it didn't get to work?

"You heard anything about how Malice's doin'?" Shatasia asked. "I know about all the broken parts. I mean, is she gonna be okay?"

"Connie says yeah. She says Malice'll be as good as she ever was."

"Ain't sayin' much," Shatasia muttered. "She comin' back?"

"Connie says no. I say good. She wouldn't come back liking us any better."

"Boo-hoo," Shatasia said. "What goes around comes around."

"You think so?"

"My gram says that, and I've seen it happen too much to think she's wrong. That's why I'm turnin' myself around. If I can. I got me some bad juju pilin' up."

"Maybe there's some so lucky or so slippery they never get caught that way, either," I said.

"Maybe," Shatasia said doubtfully. "But they're runnin' from somethin' bigger than the cops."

ELEVEN

At our next anger-management session, Nolan wanted us to talk about the men in our lives. That was a relief. We'd spent three sessions on Malice, and no matter how hard Nolan tried, we couldn't feel sorry for her. We agreed with Shatasia: what goes around comes around. But we weren't too interested in applying that to ourselves, no matter how hard Nolan tried to get us to.

"A hard man is good to find," said Andrette, a new girl now in Dahlia's single room. "The rest of them are worthless." Andrette was a lot like Sylviana: explosive, always ready to start something over the most innocent remarks. She didn't think there *was* any such thing as an innocent remark. And of course she didn't think she'd done anything bad enough to be inside, even though she'd been arrested climbing out the window of a house at ten in the morning with a revolver in her jacket and jewelry in a pillowcase.

Valencia said, "If I get another life, I want to be a man. A woman's worth nothing in this world."

Damaris nodded morosely. Revere had never come to see her. We were allowed to write ten free letters a week and she'd been writing all ten of hers to him, but he never wrote back. "The men, they got everything," she said. "They can do whatever they want with you."

"Why you let them do that?" Shatasia asked. "Why you just take it?"

"What choice I got?" Damaris asked. "I don't do what he wants, he goes."

"Well, looks like he's gone, anyway. Was it worth getting your face beat in—more than once, I'm betting."

"It was. For the good part that came after," Damaris said.

"Huh," Shatasia said disgustedly, and slumped back in her chair.

"She's right," Valencia said. "They walk if you're not good to them."

"They walk even if you are," I said. Ray had never hit me, but I knew what Damaris meant about the good part that came after a guy had been mean to you.

Valencia nodded, and so did some of the other girls. Someone added, "You're a slut if you do and a tease if you don't. And they don't like it either way. You can't win."

"How about going without a man?" Nolan suggested.

"Then who'll take care of us?" Damaris asked.

"Are these guys that you want doing such a great job of taking care of you?"

"At least then you only have to worry about one man," she said. "Not a whole train."

"How about forgetting about men for a while and helping each other?" Nolan asked. "How about depending on other women?"

"You crazy, man," Andrette said. She had three dots tattooed on the vee of her thumb and first finger that Valencia had told me stood for Mi Vida Loca. My crazy life. "You can't count on other women. They always comin' at you sideways. They steal your man. They talk about you behind your back. They tell your secrets. Women can't help you."

"Well, if you can't count on men, or depend on women," Nolan said, "who can you trust to help you when you need it?"

"Family," Valencia said, and Toozdae gave her a bleak look. I was on Toozdae's side on that one.

"Myself," Andrette said. "I'm the only one."

"Most people need more support than that," Nolan said.

"What you need and what you get are different," Toozdae said in her pale voice.

"Yes," Nolan said quietly. "It happens to all of us. Can any of you talk about how it's happened to you?"

We were still, watching him warily. Did he know our stories? Did he want to?

"Is that something that makes you angry?" Nolan asked. "Wanting what you don't get? I know it does me."

We stayed silent, but it was a restless silence, with the sense of pressure building from things not being said.

In the silence I was forced to think about what I needed and what I'd gotten. I didn't want to think about that. I wanted to be sure I didn't need anything that I couldn't supply by myself. But inside my mind, like a little e-mail, came the message that I needed someone I could call Daddy and someone I could call Mom. What I'd gotten was Dixie Lee, a brief, high-spirited presence of cowboy boots and laughter and armloads of silver bracelets. And a father both grief-stricken and angry over her, and resentful of and responsible for their daughter. When I called him anything, it was Dad, not Daddy. And Dixie Lee was just Dixie Lee.

It's true that when I was little my father bathed me and dressed me, fixed my meals, got me to school on time, took all the proper care of me. But he did it as if his mind was somewhere else, not tuned with delight just to me. It occurred to me that Ray had been the same way, and when I'd finally gotten him to respond to me, I was as jubilant as if I'd won a battle. But the work of keeping him centered on me had been exhausting and not always successful. Now both he and my father had lost interest entirely and had no intention of coming back. It made me sick with myself to realize that, even now, knowing my father and Ray the way I did, and having listened to Nolan, and having heard about Revere and other guys like him, I could still wish for someone to be good to me, even if not all the time.

"Our time's up," Nolan said. "It's okay to feel sad and angry about what you can't have. I do." He looked at us for a long moment with his kind eyes. "I'll see you next time."

I was putting the date on my journal page—May 14—getting ready to write on today's subject—"When I'm at Home I Feel [fill in the blank]"—when I realized I'd been inside just over three months. More than half my sentence had gone by. Did that mean I was getting rehabilitated? If rehabilitation meant I would never again consider doing something skaty, I couldn't say that for sure. I couldn't say if, on the outs, I would still feel so hollow and invisible that I'd need the skating to bring me to life.

With less than three months to go on my sentence, I would be getting weekend furloughs soon. It was time to think about home.

I looked at the clock and wrote: *When I'm at home I feel (1) lonely (2) angry (3) afraid (4) sad (5) trapped (6) microscopic. I wish it was a place where I felt only good things, like happy and loved, but those are feelings I never have, and especially not at home.*

That Tuesday night Barbara came into the common room after Shatasia and the others with visitors had already gone to the dining room. I'd finished my homework and was reading the latest book Kate had recommended to me.

"You've got a visitor," Barbara said to me.

Surprised, I looked up from *The Road to Oz.* I'd gotten used to reading in the evenings, especially on visitors' nights, and I wasn't sure I liked being interrupted. I was always looking ahead to the next book Kate would have for me.

"You liked *The Member of the Wedding*?" Kate had asked me when I'd finished it. "What did you like about it?"

"I—" I had to think. "I knew how she felt. You know, alone even with other people around. I got how she was so crazy to be part of the wedding. And the part where she goes with the soldier to his hotel room even when she's nervous about it, just because she didn't want to say no and be alone again. That was good." When I'd read that section, my stomach had felt the way it did before I went into the Jiffy-Spot with the gun, all quivery and excited. I'd never known a book could do that, the same way crime did.

Then Kate gave me *The Secret Garden.* I loved that, too, but in a different way. It was softer than *The Member of the Wedding*, but it had the same loneliness in it.

"Who's my visitor?" I asked Barbara.

"Says he's your father. Great-looking guy, by the way. Got blue eyes just like yours."

"Then he's probably who he says he is." I didn't get off the sofa.

"Well?" Barbara said.

"I haven't spoken to him in more than three months."

"No letters, either?"

"No."

"You can write ten a week for free, you know."

"I know."

"Don't you want to know why he's here? After more than three months, why he decided to come now?"

I knew. He was going to tell me I needed to pay my debt to society, to take my medicine, to mend my ways. Blah, blah, blah. I didn't want to hear it. But something Barbara said made me think. Why now? What had changed? Why *now*? I sighed. "Okay." I got up, carefully put a bookmark in *The Road to Oz*, and followed Barbara.

I'd almost forgotten what he looked like. I didn't remember he had so much gray in his hair—was that new, or had I been as blind to him as he was to me? He had a different haircut, very short and close to his head. That, and his bright blue eyes, and the angles of the bones in his face made him look cool and pure, like a saint or something. Just what I needed. I got to be the sinner again, and he could be an archangel, for God's sake, without even saying a word.

He stood up when he saw me, and walked toward me. I stopped, wondering if I was up to this.

He stood a couple of paces from me and didn't try to touch me. I didn't expect him to and was glad and disappointed at the same time.

"I wasn't sure you'd see me," he said.

"Here I am." I said it in a this-is-your-party-you-do-the-talking voice.

"Will you come sit down?" he asked.

I went to a table and sat and he followed me.

"So, how are things going?" he asked, taking a seat.

"All right," I said.

"You think you're making progress?"

"Progress?" I asked.

"You know. Getting rehabilitated. Isn't that what's supposed to happen in here?"

I shrugged.

His face was no longer so saint-like. He was getting annoyed. There was some satisfaction in that for me. In my book, the sinners could outlast the archangels every time.

"Well, are you trying?" he asked.

"Trying to do what?"

"To take advantage of what's being offered you." I could see the effort he was making to be patient, not to blow the visit in the first two minutes.

"You mean the opportunity to share information about sex and crime and gangs and drugs with others just like me? Yeah, I'd say I am."

He took a deep breath, trying to think of what to say next. It was hard for him. Good.

"You have a roommate?" he asked, apparently deciding to come at my situation from a different angle. He was probably trying to figure out who was being the worst influence on who.

"Yeah. She's in for assault with a deadly weapon. A gun. A .22, if it matters."

"Oh." He looked around. "Is she in here?"

"That's her." I pointed to Shatasia, who was down on the floor with Sharly, rolling a ball back and forth to her.

He watched her rolling the ball and saying, "Whee!" to Sharly. "She's a big girl," he said. "That her little sister?"

"It's her daughter."

"Oh." He thought for a minute. "How old is she?"

"Shatasia? Or Sharly?"

"Which is which?"

"Sharly's almost two. Shatasia's seventeen."

I knew he wanted to tell me to think about this: about teenage mothers without husbands, about babies without fathers. But he didn't. The effort was so hard on him that it silenced him. Finally he cleared his throat. "You doing okay in school?"

"Yeah." I almost hated to tell him that, because I knew it would please him. But it pleased me, too, and I couldn't help myself.

"Good. That's good." He was quiet then, out of ideas. He cleared his throat again. "Do you want me to come again sometime?"

"Do you want to? Why would you?"

He looked at me with those intense blue eyes. "I'm your father."

"I need a better answer," I said. I wanted Archibald Craven, Colin's father from *The Secret Garden*—the father who mourned Lilias, his dead wife, for ten years and then realized that his neglected child was the most important thing in the world to him.

"What's the right answer?" he asked.

I was silent, looking at his hands folded on the table. Finally I raised my head and said, "Not that one."

"Okay." He stood and put his hand on my shoulder, just for a moment. "Take care of yourself," he said.

"I always do."

"Okay," he said again, and left.

I stayed at the table, looking down at my own folded hands,

shaped so much like his. *Was* I taking care of myself? I didn't even know what that meant.

Why had he come? Just to check up on me? To see if I'd turned into the kind of daughter he could like?

When Shatasia returned to our room after the visitors left, she said, *"Who* was that dude with the laser eyes?"

"My father."

"No shi—I mean, no kidding. Zowee. He looks like an angel or something, like he could burn a hole right through you with those eyes." She looked more closely at me. "Yours are blue, like his, but they don't have that, I don't know what, that *strength*."

"He's stubborn, but he's not so tough. I'm a whole lot tougher than he is." But was I really? I'd always told myself I was. But for all my sins and low-down deeds, I'd never felt that I could relax, safe inside my toughness. It was more like a shield that I had to build all over again every day, and building it never got easier. His stubbornness, his immunity to me, seemed more natural. Achieved without effort.

I wanted poetry tonight. I'd gotten used to it at bedtime, lying there with the lights out. But since it was visitors' night, I wouldn't get any. There was something about it that slowed me down, that filled my mind, and the rest of me, too.

TWELVE

GRC was always quiet on Saturdays because about half of the girls were gone—on weekend furloughs or day trips with relatives. That Saturday, Valencia was with her aunt, who always brought her back loaded with prayer cards, and Toozdae was having her first weekend furlough since her mother had come back from rehab. Toozdae was both excited and apprehensive. Her mother promised that this time was different; that she had things under control. That she missed Toozdae and wanted her back and would take care of her. More than anything, Toozdae wanted to believe her. She wanted to be at home with her little brothers and sisters, and with a mother who would finally act like one. I wanted that for her almost as much as she wanted it.

Those of us who were left were on our own, the one day when all our time wasn't organized for us. True, we were always being watched, but we could take naps, do each other's hair and nails, read, watch the pre-selected videos (no violence, no sex, no bad language), play games, do laundry.

It was a long slow day. I'd gotten so used to having a schedule that I didn't like the feel of empty time. It was a job to think of ways to fill it.

Mostly I read or played *Clue* with Shatasia. I was surprised that was a game we were allowed, since Colonel Mustard was always clobbering Mr. Boddy with a lead pipe in the library, or Mrs. Peacock was using the revolver on him in the billiard room. Maybe the p.o.'s figured it was a harmless way for us to have our daydreams, not that any of us was likely to be committing crimes in a billiard room, and it was also a good mental exercise. Advanced problem solving.

I was glad when dinner and showers were over and we were in bed, waiting for our story. That night the story was about Persephone, who was kidnapped by Hades and taken to the underworld; her mother, Demeter, who missed her so much that she allowed all the crops to wither and die; and her father, Zeus, who convinced Hades to let her spend only part of the year in the underworld and the rest of the year with her parents.

I tried to imagine a mother who would pine for her daughter and a father who would argue with Hades for her.

The poem was called "Solo for a Saturday Night Guitar" and it strummed me to sleep.

I came awake and didn't know why. My bedside clock said 2:36 and the hall was quiet. But I had the sense that it was a sound that caused me to wake up frightened, something high-pitched and thin.

I got out of bed and tiptoed to the door, so as not to disturb Shatasia. Through the little window in the door I could see the hall was empty and still.

And then it came again, the high, wailing sound. The hair on my arms stood up.

Across the hall, I saw Damaris's face in the window of her

door. We looked at each other through the dark glass, like figures in a dream. Then, silently, I opened the door.

It was strictly against the rules to be out of our rooms at night, and getting caught would mean many demerits, but I couldn't help it. Something pulled me. I had to know what was making that inhuman, terrifying sound.

Damaris followed me. Together we crept to the end of the corridor as the cry came again. When we neared the door to the common area, we could hear other voices, too, urgent and sharp.

I took a quick look through the glass in the door and my heart stopped in my throat. The noise came from Toozdae. She was sitting on the floor, her battered face turned to the ceiling, her bloody hands tearing at her own hair. The front of her T-shirt was covered with blood, and she was barefoot. Barbara knelt beside her, one arm across her shoulders, the other hand trying to disengage Toozdae's hands from her hair.

With my back pressed against the wall on the other side of the door, I could see on a slant, and I could hear every word. Damaris leaned against the wall on the other side of the door, her hand against her mouth.

"Toozdae, Toozdae," Barbara was saying. "Tell me what happened. The paramedics are coming. Show me where you're hurt."

Toozdae continued to howl, her face wet and bruised, her bloody hands moving restlessly.

"He tried it again," Toozdae sobbed. "And I just couldn't. I wouldn't. I wanted to start fresh and he was going to ruin it all."

Barbara held her against her chest, smearing blood and tears onto her blouse. "It's okay," she murmured. "It's all right. Who tried what?"

Other people were moving behind them; the other p.o.'s, the night director, I don't know who.

"I wouldn't," Toozdae kept saying. "I wouldn't. He didn't believe me. He kept going. Shatasia said I couldn't take the easy way, I had to fight. So I hit him."

"Shh, shh," Barbara said, holding Toozdae's hands to keep them out of her hair. "Where did this happen? Where was your mother?"

"At an NA meeting. So I had to hit him and he got mad."

"I'll say he did," Barbara said. "Who was he? Did you know him?"

"And he hit me back. And hit me and hit me and hit me. So I ran. I ran right out the door and I didn't even remember I didn't have any shoes on. But he couldn't do it. I wouldn't let him do it."

"You came all the way here from your house on foot?" Barbara asked, incredulous. "In the middle of the night?"

"It wasn't the middle when I started," Toozdae said. "I didn't know where else to go. This is the only place I ever felt safe."

I pressed my fingers against the bridge of my nose and looked up. I had to keep pressing. Hard. Shatasia had guessed right about Mark.

Barbara wiped the back of her hand across her eyes. It left a smear of Toozdae's blood on her cheek.

The paramedics came through the doors then. There was a lot of confusion while they checked Toozdae over and then loaded her onto a gurney and wheeled her out.

Damaris and I never moved, watching it all through the window.

When Toozdae was gone, Barbara slumped into a chair, and Yolanda, the night p.o. who'd replaced Malice, huddled with her. We couldn't hear what they were saying but it didn't matter. Now somebody would do something about Mark. Now Toozdae would be free of him. But she would never get to be who she could have been without him.

Damaris and I looked at each other but didn't say anything. Then we went back to our rooms and quietly closed our doors. I wished I'd been able to go out to Toozdae, to hug her, to tell her that she had taught me something. That strength *can* grow.

I wondered if Damaris was remembering how Revere had belted her.

I don't know how the word got around. I know I didn't say anything, but by breakfast the next day everybody knew about Toozdae.

"Damn," Shatasia said. "Damn, damn, damn. I should have known somethin' would go wrong. That Mark is just pure bad news. I should have warned her, or prepared her, or *something*. We ain't just blobs that get done to. We can *do*. We got to remember that. We can *do*."

"She *did* do," I reminded Shatasia. "You told her she should fight and she did. You did help her."

"You think she remembered I said that to her?" Shatasia asked.

"I know she did."

Monday night, the bedtime story was about the Ugly Duckling. How well I knew that duckling: feeling ugly no matter what he really looked like; not having a place of his own; lonely and adrift. But it was a fairy tale, so he got a happy ending. In real life, happy endings aren't such a sure thing.

This was the closing poem:

Hold fast to dreams
For if dreams die
Life is a broken-winged bird
That cannot fly.

Hold fast to dreams
For when dreams go
Life is a barren field
Frozen with snow.

What was my dream? What would keep the snow from my field?

The next night, the poem was called "Oh Yes, My Dear, Oh Yes."

Oh yes, my dear, oh yes,
There is flint in me,
There is stone.
Were you blind, could you never guess,
Had you never known?
Could you not, long since, have foretold
In the dark and alone
There would flash an edge of fire
Where flint struck stone?

That was me. In the dark. Alone. Full of hard, cold stones waiting to catch fire and burn things up.

THIRTEEN

Wednesday, in anger management, Nolan wanted to talk about Toozdae. We'd found out that she'd be going home from the hospital, not coming back to GRC. Apparently, somebody who counted had decided she'd been punished enough. Mark was the one locked up now.

"What are you most mad about, with what happened to her?" he asked.

"That she didn't tell anybody about Mark. That she thought wishing things would change could make it happen," Valencia said.

"That Mark felt like he could do that," Shatasia said. "Why do guys think they can do that to any girl? They think they got those kind of rights any time they want them? They think they—"

"Okay, Shatasia," Nolan said, cutting her off. "I get it."

"That she had to start hooking when she was just a kid," somebody else said.

"That because she was a hooker on the street, Mark forced her to be one at home," I said. "She was practically a baby, and she was only doing what she thought she had to, not what she wanted to."

"That's an interesting thought," Nolan said. "That who we are is different from what we do. If that's so, then what *does* make us who we are?"

No one had anything to say to that. I knew I didn't think I was a monster or anything, even if I had done some bad things. Was Toozdae a bad person because she thought she had no choice except to be a prostitute?

No. I didn't believe that. Toozdae wanted to be good. She just didn't see any other way to go. It was ignorance that made her choices for her. But there were other reasons for going wrong, reasons not as innocent as Toozdae's. Dahlia's reasons weren't innocent, that was for sure. And what about mine? I couldn't be like Dahlia. So was I like Toozdae?

"Who we are is inside," Valencia said. "What we do is outside."

"How's that feel?" Nolan asked. "Being different on the inside and the outside."

"What do you mean?" Valencia asked. "Nobody shows on the outside what they are on the inside. You know what my brother calls that? Baring your throat."

"You mean like with dogs?" Lolly asked. "How they try and bite each other in the throat?"

"Yeah," Valencia said. "You don't let somebody know where it would be easy to get at you. The outside has to be the tough part."

"So you're protecting yourself," Nolan said. "Keeping your softer parts hidden. Is that right?"

"I guess," Valencia said.

"I wonder what happens to the softer parts if they never get out, never get used."

Valencia shrugged. "They're still in there."

"Can you be sure," Nolan asked, "if you never see them?"

"Where would they go?" she asked.

"Like muscles that don't get used," he said. "They wither. Then they're useless. You have to use the parts of you that you want to keep. A famous writer named Kurt Vonnegut said that we are what we pretend to be, so we must be careful about what we pretend to be." There was a long silence. Then Nolan said, "Does it make you angry, knowing you have to hide a lot of yourself? Do you think you'd be less angry if you didn't have to do that?"

"Not less angry," Lolly said softly. "Less sad. And less sick to my stomach."

"Did you know," Nolan asked her, "that sadness is sometimes anger turned inside? When there's no good place to put anger, we can turn it on ourselves."

"Yeah?" Lolly said. "You know, that's *good*. I get angry about what's happened to me, about who's done what and who hasn't done what, but so? Who's gonna care about that? Who's gonna do different? So I get sad. I can see how it works."

I could, too. What went on between me and my father was so much about anger, about who had done what and not done what. And Dixie Lee was in on it, too. Even though she was dead, she wasn't gone.

"Can you quit being sad?" Lolly asked. "Or angry?"

"Anger's not always a bad thing," Nolan said. "You're right to be angry about Toozdae. What happened to her was wrong, it shouldn't have happened. You can reduce that kind of anger by promising that next time you'll try to do something. You'll speak up, even if it's hard to do. It won't always work, but knowing you at least tried will be some help."

"What about right now?" Shatasia asked. "I'm still angry."

"Okay," Nolan said. "Be angry. It's the right way to feel in this case. Anger's only bad if it makes you do harmful things—to yourself or other people. It's funny, isn't it, how being too happy is never a problem, even when it may be inappropriate. But nobody wants to see anger, not even when it's called for. Anger makes people too uncomfortable. Well, I'm telling you, what happened with Toozdae was wrong, and it's okay to be as angry as you want to about that. I'm angry, too. I could have helped if I'd known what was happening to her. Let's let out some of that anger." He opened his mouth and bellowed, stamping his feet hard on the floor. "Come on," he yelled. "On your feet. Help me."

We came to our feet, screaming and crying and kicking our chairs.

The door opened and Connie stuck her head in. "What's going on?" she yelled over the noise.

"It's okay," Nolan yelled back. "This is for Toozdae."

Connie shut the door behind her and stood leaning back against it, and she screamed, too.

After a few minutes we had to quit. No matter how good an idea a tantrum is, you can't keep it up for very long. It's too exhausting. You get caught up in it and forget what you're yelling about and then it's not doing what it should be for you.

Connie shook her head, smiling, and left.

"Okay, everybody, well done," Nolan said. "I've been known to sit in my car in my garage with the windows rolled up and holler like that until I've had enough of being mad. It helps for a while."

"Is that all you can do when you have a lot of feelings?" I

asked. I usually didn't say much in group, but thinking about how I might be like Toozdae made me have to ask this question.

"What sort of feelings?" Nolan asked.

"Well, what if you're somebody who feels a lot of feelings and all that makes them shut up for a while is excitement. You know, that *rush* that fills you up? What if you're somebody who can't get rid of that rush even if it gets you in trouble, because it helps with the feelings?"

"Yeah," said Lolly.

Valencia's head was nodding, and so were a few others.

"Is it only crime that makes you feel that way?" Nolan asked. "That gives you enough excitement to quiet the feelings that bother you?"

"Drugs do it, too," Susan said.

"They don't do what I want," I said. "I need to feel strong and smart and fast, and I want to be able to remember. Drugs make me too out of it."

"Is feeling that you're getting away with something what's exciting?" Nolan asked. "Or is it knowing that you're pushing yourself to your limits, using everything you've got?"

"What if your biggest talent is shoplifting?" Susan asked.

"How about seeing that your biggest talent is manual dexterity," Nolan said. "That means you can play tennis or repair watches or assemble computers. Gives you a few more options, doesn't it? Makes your insides more like your outsides."

The buzzer sounded for the end of the hour.

"Nolan!" I said over the noise of chairs scraping and people moving out. "How do you know what your talents *are*?"

"We can talk more next time," he said. "But for now think about what you like to do. *Legal* things," he emphasized, and laughed.

In the free time between group and dinner, I tried to do homework, but my mind kept going back to what Nolan had said. The only legal thing I'd been doing lately that I liked was reading the books Kate gave me. Sometimes they gave me the same kind of thrill that skating did. Great. I could hardly picture myself with my nose in a book for the rest of my life.

FOURTEEN

I was eligible for my first home furlough. Connie took me aside one morning after breakfast and told me.

"You're lucky," she said. "Some of the girls have to go to relatives or older siblings or other placements because there's no one else for them. But you have your father."

Only technically, I thought, but didn't say it.

"Anyway," Connie went on, "you'll be going home for your weekend. And we'll be conferring with your dad later to see how the visit went. It's going to be fine, right?" Connie said. "Because if it's not, if there are any problems at all, your release date could be pushed back and your future furloughs will be compromised."

"Sure," I said. "Everything'll be fine." What else was I supposed to say?

Connie gave me a close look. "You do know that's what everybody tells me, no matter what strange and secret plans they actually have. You're not going to be up to anything I wouldn't approve of, are you?"

"Me? I've been impeccable in here," I said, using one of that week's spelling words.

"Anybody can be impeccable when they're being watched constantly. Think you can do it on your own?"

"Sylviana and Dahlia were being watched and they found a way to be . . . peccable."

Connie smiled. "I'll call your dad and set a time for him to pick you up. Bet he'll be glad to see you."

"He'll be wetting his pants with joy," I said.

Shatasia was going home for the weekend, too.

"You ain't very excited about it," Shatasia said, three days later, as we packed.

"Yeah, well, my dad and I aren't exactly best friends. A whole weekend alone with him sounds like a real long time."

"A whole weekend with my Sharly already seems like a real short time," Shatasia said. "I'm goin' to be tryin' to spend it all with her and not be thinkin' I need to go out with my homies. That's goin' to be the hard part for me, bein' strong against that. How about you?"

I zipped my bag shut. "I might be tempted, but I don't think I'll be hanging with the same people I did before."

"They the ones you did your job with?" she asked. Without waiting for an answer, she went on, "They won't be holdin' no grudge, you know. Not that I'm tryin' to get you to see them, but you're the one got caught, not them."

"What if I'm the one holding the grudge?" I asked her.

"Well, that's different. Then you got to watch out for wantin' to do something about it."

"Yeah," I said. "That could be a problem." I definitely hadn't forgotten about Pam, how she stayed out of a deed done with her gun, how she moved in on Ray after first dropping me out of her universe. Some friend she'd been. Sure I had a grudge.

I waited in my room for my father to pick me up. When he arrived, I went out to meet him.

"Can I carry that for you?" he asked, gesturing to my bag.

I shook my head and followed him out.

Our ride home was mostly silent, except for some remarks he made about the weather—"A little cool for this time of year"— or the scenery—"The bakery burned down since you've been . . . away."

The house that I had lived in since I was four—my father bought a new house after Dixie Lee died, not wanting to stay in the one he'd shared with her—was the only home I could remember. Yet now it looked completely unfamiliar.

"Did you paint the house?" I asked.

"No. Why?"

"The trim around the windows. Has it always been green?"

"For at least the last ten years. Don't you like it?"

"It's fine. I like it fine," I said distractedly. It was as if I was seeing my house for the first time. It was a nice little house. Why wouldn't it be, the way my father never allowed the paint to peel or the driveway to crack. I'd been thinking of it as a bad place because I'd been so miserable living there. But obviously it wasn't the house's fault.

In the living room I had the same sensation of strangeness. The colors looked brighter, the furniture bigger. The whole house seemed to have turned into a different place, where my absence had been accepted and sealed over.

My own room was a revelation, too. I hadn't noticed before how menacing the heavy-metal posters on the wall were, how spartan everything else was. No stuffed animals on the bed, no bulletin board with movie tickets or prom programs, no photographs of friends. I didn't even have a picture of Pam or Ray. It was just as well, considering the way things turned out.

I must have gotten used to having Shatasia around, with her strong opinions and her pictures of Sharly, because this room seemed too cool, too uninhabited. True, my father had made the bed and hung up the scattered clothes since I'd been gone, but the difference between my room at GRC and my room at home was bigger than just cleanliness. The room at GRC had life.

I dropped my bag on the bed and wandered into the kitchen. This I *had* missed. Being able to make any kind of snack for myself anytime I wanted. My father sat at the kitchen table, the newspaper laid out in front of him, though he didn't seem to be reading it.

"Are you hungry?" he asked. "Can I fix you something?"

I stood in front of the open refrigerator. "I'm just looking. I can take care of myself."

"Suit yourself," he said, turning back to the paper. After a pause, during which I removed peanut butter, an apple, and a bottle of cranberry juice, my father asked, "Is there anything you'd like to do? Go to a movie? Or we could get a video and some pizza if you don't want to go out."

Was he suggesting that I should stay home to keep out of trouble? Or that I should be too embarrassed by my criminal activities to go out in public? Or was he just asking an innocent question? He was treating me carefully, as if I was an armed bomb. He could so easily disarm me, if he only knew it.

I decided to let him try. While I sliced the apple, I said, "There was this girl at GRC whose stepbrother was doing things to her. Things she didn't like." I gave him a look to see if he knew what I meant, but he didn't raise his head from the

113

paper. "When she went home on her furlough, he beat her up because she wouldn't let him do what he wanted to with her anymore." I stopped, the knife in my hand, waiting for his reaction.

He cleared his throat and said, "Well, those are the kinds of people you seem to prefer."

I stabbed the knife into the peanut-butter jar. Why did he have to say that, making sure I didn't forget I was defective? Why couldn't he have heard what I was telling him? Didn't he care about what could happen to somebody like Toozdae? Like me?

I flung a glob of peanut butter onto the plate with the sliced apple, sloshed some juice into a glass, and took off for my room.

I stayed there, boring as it was, until I heard my father's car leave the driveway. He must be going for the pizza and the video, I thought, opening the door to my room. It'll probably be some G-rated junk. For sure, he wouldn't want to encourage me in my wicked ways with any movie about crime.

I wandered through the house. Why was I spending my furloughs here? This isn't where I wanted to live when I was released. Having to come back here would be worse than staying at GRC.

I began looking in drawers and cupboards, I didn't know for what. I needed to find something that would tell me what to do next, help me know what would happen to me.

In my father's room I found two rolls of quarters in his sock drawer. I put them in the pocket of my jeans. In the drawer of the bedside table were three twenty-dollar bills. I pocketed those, too. Old habits are hard to break. Besides, he owed me, big time.

He came back with two videos, one a comedy and one a family adventure, both as G-rated as they come, and a pizza with everything except anchovies.

"I didn't know what you'd like, so I got two movies and a loaded pizza. You can pick off what you don't want. I hope you weren't craving anchovies. I can't stand them."

"Whatever," I said.

We started one movie right away. It saved us from having a totally silent dinner. By the time the movie was finished, so was the pizza. While it rewound, I got up and made myself some coffee. My father cleaned up from dinner and then we sat through the second movie.

Before it was over, he was yawning like one of those snakes that can unhinge its jaw to swallow something big.

"I've had it," he said, standing and stretching.

"I'll rewind the video," I said. "You can go to bed."

"Okay," he said, heading down the hall. "Don't stay up too late."

"Right."

The video rewound. I ejected it, put it neatly in its box, and piled it with the other one on the front hall table. Whatever else he thought about me, he'd at least have to give me credit for responsible video care.

I was restless and itchy and too full of coffee to be sleepy. I missed my routine of dinner, job, homework, shower, story. I missed Shatasia. I felt trapped and empty and breathless, the way I had those first few days at Juvie. I needed to do something, but I didn't know what. And this was supposed to be the freedom I wanted so much.

I had to get out of there. Leaving the house in the middle of the night was a probation violation, I knew that, but I didn't care. I had to get out where there was air; where I wasn't surrounded by proof that my father was living so well without me. Where I could see if there was still a place I could fit in.

An hour had passed since I last heard a sound from my father's room. Carefully, I let myself out the kitchen door, pulling it closed quietly behind me.

My bike was where it had always been in the garage, covered with cobwebs. It had been years since I'd ridden it. Nobody I knew rode bikes anymore. Hadn't since fourth or fifth grade. I wasted some time finding the pump, but it was necessary since the tires were too flat to ride. After I'd pumped them up and dusted off some of the cobwebs, I wheeled the bike down the driveway. I hoped I could remember how to ride it.

It didn't take long to get the hang of it again. What a great invention, I thought, speeding along in the cool night air. Silent, small enough for me to hide easily, quick to stop and start, able to go places an automobile couldn't. Why didn't more criminals use bicycles?

FIFTEEN

Riding through the dark and vacant streets revived old feelings in me, ones I'd been hoping I'd forget: the thrill of skating, the sense of belonging when I was out with Ray and Pam and Sonny, the pleasure of Ray's attention when he turned it on me. Could anything replace those feelings? What would skating be like if I did it alone? Could I find other people to do it with who would make me part of them, fill my empty places?

Without knowing that's where I was going, I had pedaled to Pam's house. I stopped across the street. The house was dark except for the glow of the porch light. At the end of the block, a car was parked. I pedaled closer to it and looked in the window. It was Ray's. I knew it by the red-and-black garter that hung from the rearview mirror.

Was he here? With Pam in her dark bedroom? It would be just like her to smuggle him in right under her parents' noses. They would be even more offended by him than my father was, because they believed their darling Pam was perfect and deserved a perfect boyfriend.

Her bedroom window opened onto the driveway. Many times she and I had gone out through it on our way to places our parents never knew about, and back in through it later. Ray could go in and out as easily as we had.

As I stood by Ray's car, a station wagon with the radio on too loud drove up in front of Pam's house. It idled there as the door opened and two figures got out. Pam and Ray.

I could hear everything they said, even over the music. What a bonus time they'd had, what a great party it had been, lots of laughing. I almost literally saw red. Once I'd thought they were my friends. Now they were playing and partying while I was scrubbing toilets, being watched even when I was in the shower, and going to bed at ten o'clock. And I'd bet big money that they never thought about me at all.

I moved with my bike into the shadows of the house Ray's car was parked in front of.

The station wagon drove off, leaving Pam and Ray on the sidewalk.

"Come sit in the car with me," Ray said.

"Why don't we just go inside?"

"Because your father hates me."

"He's asleep. He'll never know."

"He could wake up. He makes me nervous now that he's got his gun back."

Pam laughed. "Chicken."

He grabbed her around the neck with the crook of his arm and pulled her next to him. "Don't call me that," he said, and I knew that tone of voice. I hated it, but it worked; I always did what he wanted when he talked to me like that.

"Hey," Pam said, annoyed. "No goodies for you when you treat me like that."

"There'll be goodies if I want them," Ray said, pulling her tighter against him.

Maybe getting Ray was the perfect revenge for Pam. He could mess her up with no help from me. But how would that satisfy *my* need for payback?

"Okay, okay," Pam said. "Let me go. I'll get in the car."

That's how Ray got his way: by force, or by ignoring you until you'd do anything to get him to pay attention to you again. I'd been as stupid about men as Damaris had.

Ray and Pam passed so close to me that I could smell the cigarette smoke on their clothes, but they didn't see me in the shadows. I wished I could come out then, just to see the looks they'd give me. But something held me back. I needed to see how they were together, if Ray could be different with her than he'd been with me. If they talked about me.

Ray let himself in the car and leaned across the front seat to open the door for Pam. She got in and their two silhouettes merged into one. It was obvious I was not on their minds in even the smallest way.

The front door of the darkened house I was hiding beside opened and an old dog stepped creakily out onto the porch. I moved deeper into the cover of the shadows. A barefoot man in a T-shirt and boxer shorts, scratching his sleep-tousled head, came out after the dog.

"Hurry up, Peanut," he said. "Do your business and lets us old guys get back to bed."

The man stood on the top step while the old dog made his slow way down to the front yard. He wandered stiffly around it, looking for just the right spot, sniffing vigorously.

"Come *on*," said the man on the porch. It was then that he noticed Pam and Ray in the car. "Hey," he said to himself, and started down the porch steps.

He banged on the car's passenger-side window until Pam

rolled it down a couple of inches. "Oh, it's you," he said to Pam. "Your parents wouldn't like it if they knew what you were doing out here. Why don't you go on home now? Don't ask for trouble."

Ray said something I couldn't understand, but I could tell it wasn't complimentary.

"The same to you, buddy," said the man, straightening up. "Now get out of here before I call her parents."

Ray started the car and drove off with his hand on the horn, blaring into the dark as he turned the corner.

The man made a rude gesture after him and the dog stood, head up, watching them go.

"That girl's got mixed up with a punk, huh, Peanut?" the man said to the dog. "Don't let them make you forget what you came out here to do."

Peanut remembered, did it, and he and his master went back inside.

My need for payback had evaporated in a cloud of car exhaust, and I didn't know if I was glad or sorry. What I wanted right then was to be with Ray and Pam. I knew it was crazy. Hey, I knew it was impossible. But I still wanted it. Being with them and Sonny had filled up a hole in my life. I couldn't think of anything better than being with them, the way it used to be, in those times when Ray was good to me.

I felt like Peanut, distracted and wobbly, as I rode my bike back through the dark streets to my house. Once the bike was safely stashed in the garage, I let myself in the house and fell into bed in my clothes.

It was nearly eleven when I woke up. Good. The weekend was almost over. Check-in time at GRC was four o'clock. If my father reported an uneventful visit, I'd be back here again

120

next weekend. I could watch Pam and Ray again, like looking through the wrong end of binoculars, back to my old life, searching for clues to the life I'd have next.

My father was nowhere around when I got up. It wasn't until I had a shower and was sitting at the kitchen table over a breakfast of stale Lucky Charms that must have been in the cupboard since I left that I saw him out in front, washing his car. That could take him hours, the way he went after the wheel rims with a toothbrush, and Armor All-ed the whole interior. The car should be ready just in time to take me back to GRC.

I carried my cereal bowl in front of the TV and ate while I watched cartoons. How come rabbits could blow people up and steal clothes and food from stores and it was funny? When people did it, they got locked up.

TV makes you stupid, no question about it. I hadn't had this big a dose of it since I'd gone to GRC, and I'd forgotten what a narcotic it was. I was zoned out in front of it, stoned by it, when my father came through the front door.

"Oh, you're finally up," he said, and went on down the hall without another word.

When he came back, he was holding out the rolls of quarters and the three twenties. "Would you care to tell me how these got into the pocket of your jeans?" he asked.

For a second, I couldn't remember. Then I just looked up at him and shrugged. "What do you expect? I'm a felon. And what does that make you, going through my pockets?"

"It makes me your father, Dallas. I'll have to report this, you know."

"Whatever," I said, looking at the TV cartoons. "I'm not dumb enough to think you want me to come home, anyway."

"Think about this," he said, his arm falling to his side. "If you don't come home, it won't be my fault. It'll be what you've done to yourself."

I remembered something Kate had said one day in class. Susan had asked her why she was teaching us when she could be teaching in a school of good kids.

"We all have good *and* bad in us," Kate had said. "You, too. But let's face it. None of you would be in here if you'd spent your spare time reading to your poor old bedridden grannies. And I really mean *face It*. I know you all think you got a bad rap, that you weren't doing anything so wrong, that you don't belong here. What you really mean is you're steamed that you got caught. Because you were all caught doing something you shouldn't. Don't try to fool me. I'm well acquainted with that Byzantine reasoning about how you were just *there*, but you weren't really doing anything, or how you were only holding the gun, the drugs, the stolen property, whatever, for somebody else. You had nothing to do with any actual crime, or somebody tricked you into whatever you did or forced you, and on and on. I know all those excuses. Being bad is easy. At least for a while. Until you get caught. Until you're not somebody you like. Good is harder, no doubt about it. But it makes you feel better. I want to help you feel better. Those of you that will let me. You get to choose."

She and Nolan, always talking about choices.

Well, I was choosing. Except that it didn't feel like choosing. It felt inevitable, like a tidal wave, an earthquake, something that couldn't be stopped.

And so was my father. He chose how he treated me, how he thought of me, who he wanted me to be.

"You might as well take me back to GRC now," I said.

"Is that what you want?"

"Why not? I'll go get dressed."

He walked me in and said goodbye, but he didn't touch me or even try to. He left his report form about how the weekend had gone with the receptionist before he went out the door. After watching us, the receptionist probably didn't even need to read it to know what the weekend had been like.

Shatasia was still away on her furlough. Even knowing our room was empty, I liked its familiarity, liked being back in it.

At four, Shatasia blew in. "Oh, girl, what a time! I mean it."

"What? What happened?"

She sat heavily on the bed, dropping her bag at her feet. "I had Sharly out in the yard in front, showin' her how to ride her little trike and all. We got a fence so it's safe for her. But there was people goin' by, wantin' me to go with them. The same guy was still dealin' on the corner. Some homies started fightin' across the street, sayin' words I don't want in Sharly's head. And you never know how those fights could end up. So I took Sharly inside. Later when I went out again, after everything had settled down, to get that trike, the street was quiet, nobody around, nothin' happenin'. That stuff comes up like a wind around Gram's place and then it goes away, but you can't ever get all the way relaxed again. Dallas, I *got* to get my Sharly out of there. I *got* to do better for her."

"That's rough," I said.

She fell back on the bed. "You're not kidding." Then she looked over at me. "So how was things at your place? Everything okay?"

"Sure," I said. "Pretty quiet."

"Quiet sounds good. You be goin' home again next weekend?"

"I don't know. I'm not so sure that'll work out."

"I'm hearin' you," Shatasia said, but didn't ask any more questions.

SIXTEEN

The next day at P-E, when we finished our volleyball game and still had some time left before we went in for group, Lolly asked if anybody had a jump rope.

"Hey, good idea," Connie said. "We're bored with volleyball." She rummaged in the equipment cupboard and came up with an unused length of clothesline, still in its wrapper.

"Will this do?" she asked.

"Yeah," Lolly said. "Who wants to turn?"

I volunteered. I was feeling low, the after-effect of my furlough, and jumping seemed like too much work right after volleyball. Besides, I hadn't jumped rope since I was about eight, and I could still remember the frustration of getting my feet tangled in the rope and having to keep starting over. Frustration wasn't appealing to me just then.

Valencia took the other end and Lolly jumped in. I'd never seen anybody jump rope the way she could. Her long, lanky body was made for it. She did dance steps and kicks and tapped her heels with her hands and made it look like the most fun anybody could have. When she got tired, Damaris said she'd like to do it, too, so Valencia and I kept turning.

Damaris was almost as good as Lolly, and even more graceful. When Lolly got a load of Damaris, she yelled, "You go, girl!" and clapped her hands in time to Damaris's jumping. Then she jumped in, too, and the two of them were off, dancing around each other, playing patty-cake, laughing their heads off.

Andrette had to get in then, too. She didn't want anybody to be better than her at anything.

She wasn't anywhere near as good as Lolly or Damaris, and it made her furious. And the harder she tried, the more mistakes she made, and the more she got laughed at.

Suddenly she stopped jumping, and the rope caught around her feet. She rushed up to Valencia, who'd been laughing the loudest, and knocked her down.

"Hey!" Connie yelled, running to separate them. Kate came, too, and Bobbi, a new day p.o. Andrette was crazy, whacking away on Valencia, who was whacking back. They were screaming and pulling each other's hair, while the rest of us stood there watching. Shatasia had her arms out in front of us, like a crossing guard protecting little kids, as if she could stop any of us from getting in on it if we'd really wanted to.

Kate and Connie and Bobbi pulled them apart and Connie did some kind of martial-arts hold on Andrette that made her stand up very straight, and the two of them marched off, through the doors, inside.

"I'm not forgetting about you, Valencia," Connie called back. "You and I'll be talking later."

Kate and Bobbi got the jump rope started again, and we went on as if there'd been no interruption. I guess, if you have to, you can get used to anything—even to violence breaking out, like an attack of hiccups or something, and then going away as suddenly as it started. But, like Shatasia said, you could never get all the way relaxed about it.

When the buzzer went off for group, we went in reluctantly, high on jumping rope, with Andrette's attack on Valencia already part of the wallpaper. Shatasia helped Valencia fix her hair, not an easy thing considering how big and back-combed it was, and all Valencia said was, "That Andrette, she's crazy to the curb. She belongs in the camp." And that's evidently where she went. We never saw her again in GRC.

After AA that afternoon, all anybody could talk about was how the rest of us could learn to jump like Damaris and Lolly. I wanted to, too. Even the talking-to I got from Connie about my father's furlough report didn't dent my enthusiasm.

After that, we lived for P-E. It reminded me of elementary school, where the fads came and went—jacks, roller-skating, bubble-blowing—and with each one we were passionately, obsessively involved. Until it was over. Then it was a dead fish as the new obsession took hold. But its turn would come around again, and new life would breathe into the dead fish; roller-skating would be fresh and exciting once more, we would spend hours at it, dream about it, live for it all over again.

That's how we were with jump rope, and I loved it. There was no room in my head for anything but jumping. I was eight years old again.

I could hardly believe that some of the girls had never jumped rope before. For some, there had been no safe place to do it. Some weren't in school enough to get caught up in the fads, because they were staying home taking care of little brothers and sisters, or because nobody woke them up in time to go, or because they already felt that it was a place that wasn't for

127

them. Which made them all the more excited about jumping rope now. They were like me, eight years old again.

I didn't mind at all when my furlough for that weekend was canceled because of what my father had written in his report. I was glad I could stay at GRC and work on my double Dutch. The life Pam and Ray were having dimmed in comparison.

"You know," Lolly said to me one afternoon as we went to lunch, "this jumping's doing something to my stomach."

"Making it worse, you mean?" I asked.

"No. Making it better. Maybe jumping rope's a better way to cool off my nerves than throwing up."

"Sounds that way to me," I said. "I know I'd like it a lot better."

"Maybe I was, you know, the way Shatasia's always saying, not looking hard enough for an answer. She's maybe got a point. If you do what you always do, you're going to get what you always got. So it makes sense you should try something else."

"Yeah," I said. "She's got a lot of points. And there's still times I just want her to put a cork in it."

Lolly laughed. "She can be kind of a drag, can't she, always trying to get stuff right, and make everybody else do that, too."

"I know. But I guess having a baby makes a difference. I'm just glad I don't have one."

"Me, *too*! They slow you down something awful. I've got a lot of doing yet to do."

"You're not the only one," I said, while I wondered what, exactly, my doing would consist of.

Lolly may have been a great jumper, but she was a lousy teacher. She was too good to be able to simplify what she was doing for the beginners, and she was too impatient to wait for them to catch on. All she wanted to do was jump.

To everyone's surprise, the great teacher was Damaris. She thought nothing of making everybody else wait while she slowly, patiently, calmly explained to someone something that seemed completely obvious to the rest of us, itchy and edgy, wanting to *jump*. Damaris made us wait. She didn't cut corners. She made sure the basic steps were clear before she moved on at all.

Susan, with her heavy, square body, was the clumsiest person I'd ever seen. We all groaned when it was her turn to jump. We knew we'd be standing there forever while she tangled herself, over and over, in the rope. Damaris told her the same things again and again to try to help her.

"Jump up just when the rope passes your knees."

"Jump with both feet at the same time."

"Do a little skip in between jumps, to keep your rhythm."

Susan didn't get it. She had no sense of rhythm, and sometimes we even wondered if she was *blind*, the way she'd jump when the rope was over her head instead of under her feet. But Damaris never gave up on her. The patience and acceptance that had caused her to put up with too much from Revere were the same things that made her such a stellar teacher. There was a lesson in there somewhere, I figured, but I didn't know what it was.

The bedtime stories lately had been including an Aesop's fable every night, and they left me trying to make lessons out of everything that happened. I'd lie in bed, my calves aching from so much jumping, forming lessons, like jumping rhymes, in my mind. First we labor, *then* we dance. Slow and steady gets things done. Don't count your chickens before they're hatched. You're known by the company you keep. And my personal favorite, from "Belling the Cat"—solutions to problems are easy as long as you don't actually have to *do* anything.

We worked jumping rope into so many of our daily writing assignments that Kate finally forbid it. When she gave us the topic "What Will You Be Doing in Five Years?" she said none of us could write that we'd be professional rope jumpers. Even if we couldn't write that, we loved this topic. Because every one of us thought we were going to be doing phenomenally well: good jobs, high salaries, nice cars, pretty houses, handsome guys, beautiful babies—the whole nine yards. Five years seemed far enough away for any kind of miracle to happen. The missing part, which Shatasia pointed out to us over dinner, was *how* were we going to bell that cat? Valencia said things would work out "somehow," and Lolly thought she'd become a model because she was so thin and make lots of money, and Susan was going to win the lottery. Shatasia was the only one who had taken the assignment completely seriously; she'd written out her plan.

Damaris put down her spoon. "Why you make everything so hard, Shatasia?" she asked. "Don't you know dreams are important?"

"Sure, I know it. All I'm sayin' is how to make them come true. If you want to keep dreamin', just don't pay no attention to me. Just shut your ears, cause I'm not gonna shut my mouth." She scooped up some soup and I heard her mutter into her spoon, "Win the lottery. Huh."

"You got to have a dream," Damaris said.

"What's your dream, Damaris?" I asked.

"What I wrote," she said. "The house, the babies, the nice car. That's all."

It didn't seem like too much to want. Nothing extravagant or foolish. But Damaris's face looked like she knew she'd wished for the moon with a side of fries.

And I suspected that my own rosy vision of the future, on the five-year miracle plan, was about as realistic as becoming a professional rope jumper.

SEVENTEEN

Two weeks later I was granted another furlough. When my father came to pick me up, he brought me a bag of Tootsie Rolls.

"Do you remember how much you liked those when you were small?" he asked me as we drove home.

"No."

"Well, you did. You liked the way your teeth got stuck in them and made that funny unsticking sound when you opened your mouth. And you loved the way they made your drool brown."

"Gross," I said. But his saying that made me remember. I *did* love that brown drool. How odd he'd thought of it. How odd he was telling me about it.

"Little kids like gross things," he said.

"It made you mad then," I said, remembering that, too.

"What did I know?" he said. "I thought brown drool on your clothes was a big problem. I didn't know what a big problem really was."

"So now you do," I said. "Congratulations." Somehow he always got around to letting me know what a disappointment I was. Bringing me the Tootsie Rolls had been one of those accidents that sometimes happened that got me thinking, for an instant, that things could be different for us.

"You think it makes me happy?" he asked.

"It should. You've been expecting big problems from me all my life. So you were right."

"You must know being right about something like that gives me very little satisfaction."

It had never been any mystery to me why high-kicking Dixie Lee was out driving around with the guy next door. All my father's iron judgments could have made Mother Teresa give up on trying to be good enough.

"Why did you marry Dixie Lee?" I asked him. I'd always had trouble putting the two of them together. Which one of them had made the wrongest choice?

His eyes got a far-off look, and it was a while before he spoke. "She was like . . . like champagne. But with a Listerine chaser. She was so full of life and excitement and fun. And then she pushed everything too far. She just didn't know when to quit. But I'd never known anybody who made me feel the way she did, and I wanted her. It was that simple. I was too young and too inexperienced and too optimistic."

Those days were definitely over. "Why did *she* marry *you*?" I asked.

He looked right at me and then back at the road. "That's something a lot of people were wondering. I should have wondered about it, too. I can't really tell you. Maybe she wanted somebody to support her. Maybe she wanted to try settling down. Who knows—maybe she even loved me—for a little while. I know what you think of me. I know you see me as this big dull, I don't know, *anchor*, whose main job is to see that nobody has any fun. That's what she saw, too, after a while. And any of my softness or gentleness was just an invitation to be taken advantage of. But when you were a baby you didn't think it was so much fun to have your mother gone all the time, out looking for a good time instead of having it with you. Or being so obliterated from the night before that she couldn't get up with you in the mornings. Do you know I used to come home from work and find you alone, screaming in your crib, and her gone off on one of her adventures?"

I hadn't known that. But his saying it made me feel desolate and scared, as if I had a taproot that went straight back to that buried memory.

"Maybe you admire that kind of behavior, but I don't," he said. "I wanted better than that for you."

Her genes were half of me. I could feel them pulling on me, pulling me in her direction, to what I'd always believed was an exciting, carefree, risky place. I'd thought of Dixie Lee's early death as an affirmation of those qualities—the good time was worth the consequences, regardless of who had to bear them. I'd felt a veil of tragic glamour over me since babyhood because I'd had an impetuous, fascinating, risk-taking mother.

Now I was having my own consequences, on top of Dixie Lee's, and they didn't feel so good. I minded them. Had she? If she did, why hadn't she slowed down and cleaned up? Was it because she couldn't—those naughty old genes wouldn't let her? Were my own genes that stubborn, too? How about the ones I got from my father? Were both sets inside me, reenacting my parents' life, the little Dixie Lee genes in spike heels arguing with the straitlaced Dad genes, their arms crossed firmly over their chests? Or did genes have anything at all to do with it?

Maybe it was purely bad company. Bad luck. Bad choices, as Kate and Nolan would insist.

"You practically guaranteed I *would* turn out like her," I said, furious at him and at myself and at everything. "Always letting me know you expected that, like there was no chance I'd be okay. Well, I'm not and you can take the credit."

He just shook his head, drove the car into the garage, and got out, leaving me sitting alone in the front seat.

I sat there until I heard him start up the lawn mower in the back yard. Then I let myself into the house to the accompaniment of the clatter of machinery. My father might be able to tame the grass but he couldn't tame me.

We went through the whole routine of videos and pizza again, but this time, when he went out to get them, I found no loose twenty-dollar bills in my father's drawers, no rolls of quarters, nothing worth stealing anywhere in his room.

We sat through the videos, we ate the pizza, we didn't talk.

"You want to do the rewinding?" my father asked when the last movie finished.

"Sure," I said. "Go to bed if you want to."

"Okay. See you in the morning."

"Right."

I roamed the house for an hour, and then, when I was sure he was asleep, I went out to the garage.

The bike was where I had left it, but it had been cleaned up and polished. And it was locked to the pipe that went to the water heater. So he knew I'd taken it out. It must have driven him crazy not to know whether I'd ridden it around the block or on a crime spree. Did my father really think locks could keep me from doing something I wanted to do? I took the tiny screwdriver from his tool bench, the one he used on his eyeglasses, and fiddled inside the padlock until it popped. Then I pushed the bike out to the sidewalk.

I stood across the street from Pam's house again. Everything looked the same, except that the porch light was off. Ray's car wasn't around, either, but maybe they were still out. After all, it was Saturday night. The night of the week I'd been spending playing Clue while they partied or skated.

As I stood on the sidewalk watching, the front door of the house on the corner opened and the old dog and his barefoot master came out. The dog limped down the steps, made his way to the end of the front sidewalk, and stood outside his gate, sniffing the air. Then he turned and started toward Pam's house.

His master hurried down the steps to the gate, hesitant to go any farther in his underwear. "Hey, Peanut!" he called to the dog. "Don't go that way. They may be away for the weekend, but they still won't like it if you use their lawn. Peanut!"

The dog kept going, increasing his speed slightly as he sensed the man's urgency behind him. He stepped onto Pam's lawn and relieved himself.

"Peanut," his master said in disgust, trotting down the walk. "I told you not to do that." He scooped up the dog and carried him home, then returned with a gardening trowel and a plastic bag. He cleaned up after Peanut, went back to his own house, and shut the door.

Away for the weekend. They must have used a team of wild horses on her, since that's the only way, Pam said, she'd ever go anywhere with her parents. But they would never leave her at home alone. Not with Ray around.

I got on my bike and rode back to my house, where I locked

the bike neatly to the water-heater pipe. There wouldn't be anything bad for my father to report about me this time. I'd be able to spend another fun-filled weekend with him, waiting for my midnight visit to Pam and Ray.

I recited jump-rope rhymes to put myself to sleep.

EIGHTEEN

Shatasia would be getting out soon. Nothing had gone wrong for her during her furloughs. And she wasn't taking a single chance on breaking any of the GRC rules, the way some of the girls did when they got close to the end of their time. They'd *say* they wanted to go home, but maybe they didn't mean it. But Shatasia, she was perfect every day. She meant it.

One afternoon, while the rest of us were talking about sex with Soledad, she went to a discharge interview that included getting the Norplant put into her arm.

"I know everything I want to about sex," she said. "And a few things I wish I'd never heard of. Now I want to know about gettin' out. Tell me if you learn anything new."

The funny part was, I had learned some new things from Soledad, and I thought I already knew everything, just like Shatasia did. I'd learned about ovulation, and ectopic pregnancies and genital warts, and a bunch of other things, too. A lot of what I'd learned made me glad I didn't have to deal with guys again for a while yet.

That day Soledad wanted to talk about rape.

"So who can tell me what rape is?" Soledad asked.

"Some guy who jumps on you from out of the bushes," Susan said.

"What if it's some guy you know?" Soledad asked.

"Oh," Susan said. "A guy I know. Then it's not rape."

"No?" Soledad said. "Why not?"

"Well, he *knows* me," Susan said, in an impatient tone.

"So you're telling me that any guy who knows you can have sex with you anytime he wants to?"

"Well, yeah," Susan said, puzzled. "You telling me he can't?"

"Anybody else want to answer that?" Soledad said.

"I been here a long time," Valencia said. "I know you say rape's when you don't agree to it. And that's what all your books say. But, in real life, the guys I know don't call that rape."

"So when is it rape to them?" Soledad asked.

Valencia shrugged. "I guess when they don't know you. They sure don't notice when their homegirls say no."

"All of them?" Soledad asked.

"Maybe not *all*," Valencia said. "But a lot."

"All the ones I know," Susan said.

"You in a gang?" Soledad asked.

"Why?" Susan asked back, defiant. Of course she was in a gang. How could that be a secret when its tattoos were all over her?

"Do your homegirls look out for you? Your homeboys?"

"Sure," Susan said. "They'd kill for me."

"And your homeboys don't want to have sex with you? They're like your brothers?"

Somebody else in the room laughed and said, "Brothers can do things you don't want them to do, too. Like Mark and Toozdae."

Susan twisted in her chair. "Well, they're not exactly like brothers. They're guys, too."

"Okay, never mind," Soledad said. "My point is that consent is *always* the issue. Even if the guy doesn't think it's rape. Even if you're out of it on drugs or alcohol, though I don't recommend that as a social strategy. If you don't agree to sex, then it's rape. You don't have to kick and fight and be overpowered, either. Sometimes a woman is too intimidated or too scared to fight. But if you don't want to and you say you don't want to, and a guy still has sex with you against your will, it's rape. Whether he thinks so or not. And you can always call the cops about it."

Susan laughed. "Right. And get beat up on *top* of getting raped. If I called the cops, I better be calling Trailways next and getting as far away as I can get cause the guy and his road dogs would be on me."

"I know," Soledad said, sighing. "That could happen. But it would be wrong. What I'm telling you is the straight stuff and I want you to know it, even if that's not how it always works out."

Shatasia was in our room looking at Sharly's picture when I got back from sex ed.

"Won't be long before you can see her all the time," I said.

"Longer than I want," Shatasia said. "I'm goin' to a group home from here."

"Not to your grandmother's?"

"No. They think it's not a good place for me to be livin' permanently—in the same neighborhood as where I got in trouble, the same people waitin' to pick up with me again."

"But will you pick up with *them*?" I asked.

"While I'm in here, it's easy to say I won't. Might be harder when I'm on the outs. I grew up with most of those folks. Stayin' away from them's not something I've ever done. Just the weekends are hard enough. All I want to do is play with Sharly, but I can tell things are poppin' outside and I get curious, even at the same time that I'm jumpy about it."

"Can you have Sharly in the group home?"

"She'll keep stayin' with Gram, but I can see her every day if I want. I just can't sleep at Gram's. Then, in a few months, when I'm eighteen, I can get my own place and have her back."

"That'll be great," I said. "I bet you can do it."

"I'm scared, and that's the truth," she said. "All I want for Sharly, I got to be the one to give it to her."

"Do you remember the poem we had last night with the bedtime stories?"

"I can't remember them the way you do. How do you do that?"

"I don't know," I said. "I just do." The poems stuck in my brain without any effort, as if there was an empty spot just waiting for them to arrive. "That poem last night, that was for you."

"Tell me."

" 'In me the quiet or the strife,
In me the dying or the life,
In me the lethargy or will,
In me the power to heal my ill,
And when my soul is parched with pain,
In my own heaven the fragrant rain.' "

"Yeah," Shatasia said softly. "All that's in me, all mixed up. I wish I was sure I had a heaven with some fragrant rain."

"I think you do," I said. "And if I can, you know, help you make it rain, I'll try."

"You would? How?" She turned away and I wondered if I'd insulted her by making her feel that, by herself, she couldn't do what she wanted, the way she wanted to do it. I'd said too much and was sorry I'd started this conversation. But I believed in Shatasia's strength. I knew she had a chance, even if the rest of us, too weak, too unmotivated, too lazy, didn't. And I had to answer her question.

"I don't know how. Maybe I could talk to you, tell you I know you can do it. Or I could baby-sit Sharly. Or . . . oh, I don't know."

She didn't say anything for a long time. Just stood with her back to me.

"Sorry," I said finally, to end the silence. "I didn't mean you couldn't . . ." I trailed off. "Sorry."

Shatasia turned around. Tears brimmed in her eyes. I felt them rise in mine, too, and I raised my hand to pinch the bridge of my nose. The tears came anyway. Mortified, I bowed my head, blinking hard. I felt stupid and weak and angry at myself for starting all this.

"Hey," Shatasia said. "It's okay. I like what you're sayin'."

I looked up.

"Girlfriend, we a couple of sorry characters," Shatasia said, and wiped a tear from her cheek with the flat of her hand.

I sniffed, and so did Shatasia, and we laughed together.

NINETEEN

I always tried to write on the topics Kate suggested. It was interesting to see what thoughts wound up on the paper. Things I didn't even know were in my head. Some days the writing felt like the screaming we had done with Nolan about Toozdae—a relief and a release, even if it was only temporary. Some days the writing was hard; I couldn't get hold of what I thought, no matter how I stabbed at it or sneaked up on it. Some days the writing was easy and fun—it just flowed out of me. And I knew that, whatever I wrote, however bad my thoughts or my punctuation, Kate was the only one who would see it and she wouldn't judge me.

The day after my talk with Shatasia Kate gave us the first assignment I couldn't do. It was "Write Five Wonderful Things About Yourself."

I couldn't think of even one. That would please my father, I imagined. He'd be happy to know that at last we agreed on something. He'd said I couldn't have my furlough that weekend because he had plans he couldn't change, but maybe it was really because of what we agreed on.

Later, I asked Shatasia what she'd written. She held up her fingers. "I been thinkin' hard on this, so I was ready," she said.

"One, I got a beautiful baby girl. Two, I'm a good dancer. Three, I got long, curly eyelashes. Four, I'm young enough to make big changes for the rest of my life. And five, I'm goin' to. What did you write?"

"Nothing," I said. "I . . . I couldn't think."

"You better start," she said, in her bossy way. "You got to be your own friend, girl. If *you* can't find something to like about you, who else is gonna?"

The next day, our writing topic was "The Police: Friends or Foes?" I wanted to write about yesterday's subject. I didn't care about the police right now.

I put a big number 1 on my paper and sat staring at it. I wrote: I like my eyes. They're a nice shade of blue.

Okay. That was a start. There was at least one good thing about me. I made a big number 2 and wrote: I'm smart. I may not always act like it, but I know I am.

Number 3 came easily: I have manual dexterity. Nolan would like that: I hadn't actually been a talented shoplifter, I had just been practicing my manual dexterity. That might not be the kind of wonderful thing Kate was looking for, but it would have to do.

Then I wanted to write: I know I have a good future. But I didn't think that was true.

I wanted to write: I know I'm a good person, in spite of some of the things I've done. But I wasn't sure about that, either.

I wanted to write: I'm not going to be just like Dixie Lee, no matter what my father thinks. But that wasn't a wonderful thing. It was just a thought, an idea. Once I actually did it, it could be a wonderful thing.

"Kate," I said when I was finished. "I want you to teach me something."

"What the heck do you think I'm trying to do, every single darn day? You want to make me feel like a failure?"

When she said that, it made me wonder if Dixie Lee had thought about teaching me things. I wondered if she would feel like a failure if she could see me now.

Kate gave an exaggerated sigh. "I just hope what you want is nothing to do with quantum physics, because I'm not good there."

"You're safe," I said. "I want you to teach me to whistle through my teeth, with my fingers in my mouth, the way you do." It was the best way of getting somebody's attention I'd ever seen, next to holding a gun on them.

She laughed. "Well, okay," she said. "It's not in the curriculum, but we can work on it at P-E if you can tear yourself away from the jump rope."

Kate taught me her whistle while I watched the others jump rope and chant as they jumped:

I won't go to Macy's anymore, more, more
There's a big fat policeman at the door, door, door
He grabs me by the collar
And makes me pay a dollar,
So I won't go to Macy's anymore, more, more.

TWENTY

School was over for that day, and Shatasia was packing to leave for the last time.

"I got kind of used to this place, you know?" she said. "It's gonna seem funny not to have buzzers goin' off, tellin' me when it's time to do things."

"You'll be able to figure out when to do things," I said.

"I hope I'll be able to figure out when *not* to do things, too," she said.

"Think of me in here, listening to the buzzers. That'll help you remember not to do things."

"Yeah," she said. "Cause if I mess up I won't be comin' back here. I'll be goin' to the real thing once I'm eighteen."

"You're never leaving Sharly again," I said. "Remember?"

"I remember," she said, and zipped her suitcase closed. "You goin' to come see me when you get out?" she asked, not looking at me.

"Sure," I said. "Just make sure I know where you are."

"I'll write you. And I'll send you my phone number soon's I know it, so you can let me know what's goin' on here without me."

Connie stuck her head in the door. "Your ride's here, Shatasia."

Shatasia picked up her suitcase and tucked her stuffed rabbit under her arm. "You be good, girlfriend," she said to me. "I mean *real* good."

"I know what you mean," I said. "You, too."

"Okay." And she left, without looking back.

I sat on my bed with my arms around myself. I remembered, when we first arrived, Damaris saying she'd never slept in a room by herself. Except for sleep-overs with Pam, which usually didn't involve much sleeping, I'd never slept in a room *with* someone else. Not until Shatasia. With her, I'd gotten used to the sounds of another person breathing at night, to having someone to talk to as soon as I woke up in the morning and last thing before I went to sleep. At home I'd loved being alone in my room, and now I couldn't stand it.

Already I missed Shatasia. I felt adrift without her. Her strong vision of her future was hypnotic to listen to. She made cleaning up sound like such a good idea. She made it seem possible. Listening to her got me thinking maybe I could make plans, too, if I ever felt like it. Now that she was gone, I saw that what I'd thought was only a reflection from her. None of it came from me.

Connie stuck her head back in the door. "You okay?" she asked.

"Sure," I said, with a shrug, being cool. "I suppose I'll miss her."

Connie came in and sat on Shatasia's bare mattress. "Me, too," she said. "She had majigney-foofoo."

"She had *what*?"

147

"Majigney-foofoo," she said, laughing. "It's a word my sister and I made up. It means . . . oh, inner strength, I suppose. Intestinal fortitude. My sister and I had to have plenty of it, the way we grew up, but *inner strength* sounded so serious and pretentious, and all we wanted was something to keep us going, something that sounded like we could do it. Majigney-foofoo was perfect."

She laughed again, and so did I.

"Well, whatever it is," I said, "you're right. Shatasia's got it. So you think she'll do okay?"

"I hope so. She's got a good chance. And much as I think getting pregnant at fourteen isn't a good idea, in her case Sharly is what'll keep her clean, if anything can."

"If anything can?"

"Backsliding's pretty easy. Those old temptations call hard and loud to you, and yielding to them takes no effort at all."

"Yeah," I said, and added, "You sound like you know what you're talking about."

"You know anybody who hasn't yielded to temptation? For some people, taking another piece of German chocolate cake feels like as big a sin as sticking up a Jiffy-Spot might to you." She gave me a sideways look. "It's all in what you get used to doing. Habit's a big part of the criminal life, and habits are hard to break. I wish she could have stayed here longer. Then we could have made more progress, hammered in those good habits."

I remembered the way I'd taken my father's quarters and his twenty-dollar bills. I didn't need them. I didn't have any plans for using them. I took them because I was in the habit of taking things, of getting the charge that went with that. Except for using the gun, and the excuse of needing to buy false IDs, it was the same way with robbing the Jiffy-Spot: a habit. One that was making my life the life of a criminal. A life I was used to. And usually liked.

"What makes you think a bad habit can be broken for good?" I asked. "Isn't it always lurking around, waiting to come back at you?"

"Yeah, it is. You just have to make a new habit that's as strong. And remember how the bad habit makes you feel about yourself, even if you're getting away with it." She stood up. "Your new roommate will be arriving this afternoon."

"Who?"

"Her name's Roma, and"—she held up her hand with her palm facing me—"you know I can't tell you why she's coming here."

"She probably didn't really do anything," I said, with a straight face. "She's only here because the criminal justice system is all messed up."

"She'll no doubt agree with you," Connie said, and winked at me. "You and she can talk it over."

At the NA meeting that afternoon, I barely listened as the others went on and on about the drugs they'd taken, and when, and how, and how much, and why. I'd heard it all before. I was lucky drugs hadn't gotten hold of me, and I knew for a fact that being lucky could be better than being smart.

After group I went back to my room, and Roma was there, unpacking.

She was beautiful. More like a model or a movie star than a bad girl like the rest of us. Her hair and eyes and skin were all variations of a caramel color: she looked warm and glowing, like a low fire. Her shirt and slacks were a raspberry shade that exactly matched her lipstick.

"Hi," I said. "I'm Dallas."

"Roma," she said, giving me the briefest glance.

"Need any help?" I asked.

"No," she said. "I'm fine."

I watched her for a while. "Your outfit's pretty," I said.

"Thanks."

I watched her some more. "Dinner's at six."

"Yeah. I know."

Okay. I could take a hint. I picked up *To Kill a Mockingbird* and lay back on my bed to read. When I read it, I could be motherless Scout, and I got to have Atticus Finch for my father. A pretty good deal.

When the buzzer sounded, Roma opened the door and went off down the hall without waiting for me. Well, there was no law she had to. And even if there was, she'd probably break it.

I sat with Damaris and Lolly at dinner. Roma sat across from us like a princess among savages. She answered questions— name, age, where she lived—as briefly as possible and volunteered nothing.

Maybe she was just shell-shocked, the way I'd been when I first arrived at Juvie, thinking it was all some nightmare and that what I'd done had been misunderstood and that I wasn't like everybody else in here. And I hadn't even been somebody whose lipstick matched her outfit. Maybe the shock was bigger for someone like that.

A strange feeling came over me when I remembered that I wouldn't have Shatasia to trash Roma with before I went to bed, to listen to the bedtime story with, to call me *girlfriend*. It was the same feeling I'd gotten when my father told me how Dixie Lee had left me alone at home when I was a baby.

In our room after dinner, I tried again with Roma. "We have bedtime stories at nine," I said. "Real ones. Somebody reads on the P-A system. Kind of a weird idea, but I like it."

"I know," Roma said. "I've been here before."

"You have?" The only other person I knew who'd been here before was Dahlia, and that was no surprise to me. But Roma looked like a debutante—she was one I *could* have believed was inside by mistake. And she'd done things bad enough to get in here twice?

"That's what I said, isn't it?" she snapped. She took an emery board from her drawer and began filing her nails. "It's not that bad a place," she added. "All it does is take you out of your life for a while. You can get right back into it easy once you're on the outs."

There was a part of me that was glad to hear that, but I kept quiet about it. "I thought the idea was *not* to do that," I said.

"That's *their* idea," she said, and blew on her nails. "It doesn't have to be yours."

"You don't mind being locked up?"

"It's a little boring, but now and then you need a rest, you know? Being so down all the time can wear you out. But it's *too* boring. After a while, I need the street again."

"So your trick is not to do anything that could get you put away for a real long time?"

"The other trick is having a father rich enough to buy you good lawyers," she said. She opened a bottle of raspberry nail polish and stroked it onto her nails.

"What if he gets tired of doing that?"

She shrugged. "I'll worry about that if it ever happens. Right now he's still too pissed at the judge who referred to me as 'the cream of the crap.' " She looked at me out of the corners of her eyes. "Don't worry. I'll be the model inmate. I don't want to be here a day longer than my sentence. And just in case you're worried, I'm not in here for anything violent like some of those losers. I made and sold false IDs. It was really more of a business than a crime. It required plenty of skill and brains." She blew on her nails. "I'm not a menace to society."

"Nobody in here thinks they're a menace to society," I said. Roma looked up at me. "You think we are?"

"What do you care what I think?" I'd had enough of Princess Roma. I didn't mind sharing space with druggies, dealers, prostitutes, robbers, and assaulters, as much as I minded sharing it with Roma, her clean crimes, and her snotty attitude. I didn't want to think about how we'd been on both sides of the same crime: she making false IDs, me robbing a Jiffy-Spot for money to buy some.

During the bedtime story—*Ali Baba and the Forty Thieves*—I thought about being a menace to society. The things I'd done had been for *me*, for the connection with Ray and Pam and Sonny, and for the thrills. I hadn't thought how they affected anybody else. What harm had I really done? So I scared somebody now and then. Stealing things—a car ride or a meal or an outfit wasn't a very big deal. Beating people up, the way Shatasia and Dahlia had done—that was serious. Selling drugs to kids, yeah, you could call that a menace, but I'd never done that. Maybe I was bad, but I didn't see how I was a menace.

What I saw as the biggest actual menace to society was guys like Mark who could hurt somebody like Toozdae; women like Toozdae's mother who couldn't stick up for her kid because she herself was too gone on drugs, or Shatasia's mother who wasn't even around, for the same reason; guys who thought they could have sex with anybody they wanted and not call it rape. Fathers like Sharly's who weren't interested in their kids. Even fathers like Roma's who acted as if she hadn't done anything when she had.

Fathers like mine, who made sure I never forgot what he thought of me.

Why weren't *they* somewhere paying for the messes they'd caused? They started it all.

Would Nolan buy that? Probably. As far as it went. Then he'd start making remarks about how the things we bad girls had done were against the law. And did we think we *had* to do illegal things, or could we make choices about how we behaved? Could we really get away with blaming what we did on what our parents or our homies had done? What did we think laws were for, anyway? Just to make fun harder for us to have, or did they have something to do with preserving civic stability?

Oh, I could hear him, all right. Better than I wanted to. And having his voice in my head wasn't something I'd known had happened. I wondered how to gag that voice. I didn't want Nolan whispering in my ear for the rest of my life any more than I wanted my father's voice doing the same thing.

As I slid into sleep, I wondered why Nolan and my father, who both had the same ideas about conducting yourself, could sound so different when they whispered to me.

TWENTY-ONE

Roma was a terrible roommate. There were none of the laughs or long talks that Shatasia and I had had. She hardly talked at all, and when she did, she treated me, and all of us, as if we were feebleminded. She wouldn't even try to jump rope, which made Lolly furious. Princess Roma just sat on the sidelines, immaculately dressed, with that little smile on her face and that inward look. She never spoke up in group, either, even when Soledad or Nolan or anybody else asked her something. She would just smile that annoying smile and say, "Whatever you said, that sounds fine."

We hated her. Especially Lolly, who thought jump rope was the cure for everything, and took it personally when Roma wouldn't jump. Even though Roma was inside, too, like the rest of us, she tried to make us feel that she was there on some personal whim.

One night after dinner, when Damaris and I were washing tables, she asked me, "What's the story with that Roma? Who she think she is?"

"Not one of us, that's for sure," I told her. "She's just relaxing in here, like it was a hotel, waiting to get on the outs again and go back to what she was doing before."

"You mean, she *wants* to go back to banging?"

"That's what she says. Why? You don't?"

"Well, we're not *supposed* to. That's what they keep telling us. It's bad for us."

"You think it really is?" I stood with the sponge in my hand, waiting for her answer.

"Sure. Don't you? I listen to Nolan. I don't want who I am to be as low as what I do anymore."

"But do you think we can really do that?" It was a question I kept asking myself, trying to find if the formula existed that would make staying straight possible and interesting, and easy, and not make me feel like I was missing something.

"I hope so," she said. "Being in here, I got to like having things be neat, and eating dinner at the table, and feeling like Toozdae said, safe."

"What about Revere? You don't want him anymore?"

"Girl, he *hurt* me. I know I thought it was okay for him to do that then, but I don't now. I was scared of him mostly. I hope Nolan knows what he's talking about and there's some good men out there. I'm going back to church when I'm on the outs. Maybe that's where they are. Don't look so gloomy, Dallas. Just do one day at a time, like they say in the AA group, and the NA, too. Sometimes one hour at a time's the best you can do."

I never thought I'd be getting a pep talk from Damaris. When we first arrived, I would have bet she didn't have any chance on the outs. I'd have bet that she'd be back dealing drugs the day she left here, if that's what Revere told her to do. Now she sounded strong. Rehab, whatever it was, had worked with her.

"When do you get out?" I asked her.

"Eleven days," she said. "I got to be ready."

．　．　．

Damaris and I returned from our furloughs at the same time the next Sunday afternoon. I was furious because my father had taken us to his brother's cabin at the lake for the whole weekend. My aunt and uncle were there with their kids the first day, a day I spent mostly by myself in a canoe in the middle of the lake to avoid everybody. The second day my father went fishing but I had to stay inside because I was so sunburned. I'd brought *Little Women* to read but got too disgusted with that bunch of goody-goodies to finish it. I wanted to be at my father's house, where I could take my midnight bike excursion, spying on Pam and Ray, who were still having the life I'd had to give up.

"How was your weekend?" I asked Damaris.

"Okay," she said glumly. "Yours?"

"The same," I said. "I got sunburned."

"I noticed."

"You see Revere?"

"Didn't want to, but I did."

"And?"

"He talks pretty, I'll say that for him."

"He's missing you?"

"That's what he says. You think it's so?"

"What about how he never answered any of your letters?"

"Says he was busy."

I thought of Ray. He'd been busy, all right. With Pam.

"What if he does miss you?" I said. "Doesn't mean you have to do anything about it."

"True," Damaris said. "I don't. Wonder how he'll like that?"

"Just don't be standing too close to him when you tell him," I said.

Damaris laughed. "Good idea. You think you're ready?"

"Yeah," I lied. "Do you?"

"I think. I hope. I liked seeing my family. My friends. I didn't want the street. Not then, anyway. One day at a time. You know."

"You'll be fine."

We went to our rooms to unpack. I got permission to soak in the one tub with baking soda in the water to help my sunburn.

A few days later, Damaris left. She had an after-school job in a bakery waiting for her. It was supposed to give her something to do besides hang on the street with her homies.

Sixteen days later, Valencia told us—she said she'd heard it from Lupe, a new girl who'd been in Juvie the day before—that Damaris had been picked up again on drug charges and was in Juvie, waiting for her court appearance.

"Are you sure it's really Damaris?" I asked. "I just don't think so. She said she'd never do that again."

"How many Damarises you think there are?" Valencia asked. "It's her. She tested dirty and she was dealing. You didn't really think she was going to clean up, did you?"

"Yes," I insisted. "Yes, I did think that. She was determined."

"We can all sound like that," Valencia said. "Any time you ask us. We all think we'll stay straight, long as we're saying it from in here. Out there's different. How alone do you want to be?"

"What do you mean?"

"What are we going to tell our homies once we're on the outs? Sorry, I can't come by your place, I have to say my prayers? Sorry, I can't go anywhere with you, I'm shining my halo? Sorry I can't get bumped up with you, I'm too pure? Can you do that?"

It wouldn't be a problem for me right away, since nobody would be asking me those things. "But Damaris was sure she'd make different friends, friends from work," I said. "The way they tell us to."

Valencia laughed. "I don't know where I'm going to find any new friends. My homies'll be waiting for me, ready to go again."

"So you don't think you can stay clean?"

She shook her head, with its pile of shellacked black hair. "Even if I try, I don't think so. So why try? All it does is make things harder."

"That's what Roma says. She's just in here for a little time-out before she goes back to the same life. She *wants* it that way."

"I can't say I want it that way," Valencia said. "I just know myself and what I can do. I'm a weak person, not a bad one. Not like Sylviana. I let people tell me what to do and I can't stop myself. I don't know why. I just go and do it, too, even when I know it's a bad idea. At the time, I want to be part of everybody else. I want to do what they do. It'll get me in trouble again, I know it will, but I can't help it."

She reminded me of Frankie Addams in *The Member of the Wedding*, wanting to belong to *something*, just wanting that so much.

Or maybe she reminded me of me.

Shatasia wrote to me in her round handwriting, the i's dotted with little circles. She didn't like the group home. There were five other girls there, who competed and cut each other down, who broke the rules and dissed the houseparents. One girl had run away two days after Shatasia arrived.

"It's worse than GRC," Shatasia wrote. "Makes me wish I

was back inside, except I know it's putting me closer to Sharly. I go to school and do my work and keep myself quiet. It's hard. I miss the bedtime stories and the poetry, but I think about the fragrant rain. And I'm waiting for you to come see me. How about you call me when you can? Here it's 624-6573 and at Gram's it's 298-6282."

I went right to Connie for permission to call her.

"Hey," I said to Shatasia. "You're out and I'm in. Which is worse?"

"Hard to say, girlfriend," she said in a gloomy voice. "I feel like I need a vacation from bein' me."

"I hear you," I said.

I told her about majigney-foofoo and it made her laugh. Then she had to hang up because it was time for her to go see Sharly.

I stood by the phone, dissatisfied and lonely. I hadn't had a chance to tell her about Roma or what Valencia had said or any of the GRC gossip. I felt as unconnected as the telephone.

Connie asked me how my furloughs had been going. "No more problems with stealing, I see. Everything else okay?"

"No problems," I said. "We watch a lot of videos. It's easy to avoid arguments when you don't talk."

"Maybe your dad doesn't know what to say. A lot of men are that way."

"Well, I don't have anything to say, either. He's the grownup. He should know. And I don't want any more of those sermonettes he likes to deliver."

"He's still taking you home," she said. "That's more than some of the other girls have."

"Fine," I said. "They can have him. I want to be more than just somebody who's making her father feel uncomfortable."

"What he's feeling might be guilt."

"Oh, right," I said. "He thinks *I'm* the guilty one, remember? I'm going to grow up to be just like my no-good mother. And even if he does feel guilt, he's not doing anything about it."

"He takes you home. Watches videos with you."

"It's not enough."

"Could be a start."

"It's not enough," I said again. "Quit trying to make me think it is." Then I asked the question that had been on my mind ever since Toozdae left. "Connie, do I have to go home when I get out of here?"

She watched me, and finally said, "It's the preferred placement, unless something's going really wrong at home." I knew she was thinking of Toozdae, too. "And, as you know, that's not foolproof even when we think everything should go well and so do the families. You can make a request, a petition, to avoid going home, but space in foster homes and group homes is so limited we prefer to save it for people who really need it. Are you saying you'd rather not go home?"

"I'm thinking about it."

"Well, we need to get the paperwork going if that's what you're thinking. You'll be getting out soon."

"Twenty-two days," I told her.

"I'll see about starting the process, if that's really what you want to do. You'll still be on probation, so you'll need to be somewhere that encourages you in the right direction. You sure home's not the right place?"

If encouragement to do right was all that was necessary,

home got a gold star. Plenty of encouragement to do right there, no doubt about it. But I couldn't take any more of my father's silent, and out-loud, blame, his disapproval, his discomfort with me. I'd rather live on the street than with somebody who thought so little of me.

TWENTY-TWO

After anger management one Wednesday, Nolan asked me to stay. "I've got something to show you," he said.

"What?" I asked, watching the others leave. Susan was the last one out and she shut the door behind herself.

He dropped a book on the desk. *A Guide to Texas.*

"What's that for?" I asked. "You taking a trip?"

"No," he said. "You are."

"I'm going to Texas?" Was I being deported in some new kind of program to keep me away from my old habits?

He laughed. "No. You *are* Texas. And the trip you're taking is when you leave here and start traveling on a new road."

"What do you mean, I *am* Texas?"

"Well, look at your name. Dallas. I know you think it describes you—tough and hard and butt-kicking. I thought you might want to see what Dallas is *really* all about." He flipped through the pages, reading snatches. ". . . hot and cold . . . wet and dry . . . haute Southwestern cuisine and Tex-Mex cooking . . . rodeos and the Van Cliburn International Piano competition . . . rattlesnakes and golden eagles . . ."

"Okay, okay," I said. "What's your point?"

"My point is that you, as Dallas, can be anything you want.

You're not doomed to only one direction. Listen to the descriptions of Dallas: '. . . Manhattan of the Southwest . . . the Cadillac of Texas towns . . .' Wouldn't you rather be that than armadillos and livestock shows and tequila with a worm in the bottle?"

"I don't know," I said, giving him a hard time. "Beer and pickup trucks and hound dogs sort of suit me, don't you think?"

"I see you more as kangaroo-skin cowboy boots, frosty margaritas, and a limo with long horns as a hood ornament. You know, classy, but with attitude."

I had to laugh. It wasn't such a bad way to be described, I thought. Classy, with attitude. Better, anyway, than stupid, with attitude.

"I'm going to think of you as an oil heiress rather than a good old girl looking for trouble," Nolan said. "If that's okay with you."

"Think of me any way you want," I said. "It's a free country. I gotta go now. Adios."

There was another letter from Shatasia waiting for me.

Hey, Girlfriend,
You got to get out so I'll have somebody to talk to. Nobody here is like you was. I haven't said that "b" word yet, but I can feel it coming, now I know not Connie or Barbara's going to give me a hard time about it.

I wanted to talk to Shatasia right *then*. I didn't know what I'd say to her, but I wanted to hear her voice. Connie let me use the phone and I dialed the group home. The person who answered told me Shatasia was at her grandmother's, but when I called there, there was no answer.

I banged the phone down. Why couldn't I ever have what I wanted when I wanted it? I didn't even ask for anything that outrageous. No castles or princes or flights to Mars. Just somebody to be there, paying attention.

I picked up the receiver and banged it down, hard, a couple more times.

The next afternoon, I didn't have time to call Shatasia again. I had to go for a discharge interview with the director of the Center and a social worker and a probation officer. I was going to tell them whatever they wanted to hear, say anything I needed to say, to get myself out of here. Without Shatasia, being at GRC wasn't any different than being at home with my father. I may not have been a great, Pam-class liar, but I knew I was good enough to get myself released on schedule.

"What, if anything, is different now that you've been in rehab for almost six months?" the director asked me.

If I'd wanted to tell the truth, I'd have said: I've read a lot of books. I've gotten attached to somebody else's kid. I have Nolan whispering in my ear more than I want. But that's probably not what they meant.

"I'm not avoiding the question," I said when I could see I'd been silent too long. "I'm just thinking." I took a deep breath and started lying with sincerity. "Okay. When I came here I didn't think I'd done anything very wrong. Not enough to be put away for six months. Now I think I was doing a lot of things that didn't seem very wrong to me but weren't good, either. And I was going to do more, and they were probably going to get worse. I can't imagine I'd ever do anything violent, but now

I see how unexpectedly that can happen, too." I looked at the director, my eyes wide with candor.

The social worker spoke up. "Does that mean you think you can change how you were acting?"

"Doesn't everybody answer yes to that, just so they can get out?" Oops. A little honesty popped out there. Got to be careful with that.

The social worker frowned, but the probation officer stifled a smile and the director shook her head.

"So your answer is yes?" the director asked.

"My answer is, maybe. Or, I think so," I said. Back to solid lying. It was safer. "I've seen what happens when some of the others have gotten out. I know it's hard."

"What do you think you can do to help yourself?" the social worker asked.

I knew all the right answers. "Stay away from my old friends, stay in school, keep busy with good things, do what I'm told." Did they really think that somebody who was used to doing whatever she wanted could do all that?

"It's not easy for anybody," the director said. "And harder for you wards. But I see that you've done well here, so you know something about self-discipline."

"Something," I agreed.

"How do you feel about being inside?" the probation officer asked me.

I took a deep breath and started. "I know a lot of the girls say they hate it and they can't wait to get out and they're never coming back, but it hasn't been that bad for me. Sure, I'm tired of the scenery and I don't like all the squabbling and fighting, and some of the girls are pretty scary; that's true. But it's not so bad in other ways." I hoped they would interpret that as meaning thank you for putting me into this wonderful place where I can change my entire life and personality and become a solid citizen.

"What did you like most about the rehabilitation experience?" the social worker asked, as if it was a new ride at Disneyland.

"The bedtime stories," I said. "Whoever had that idea should get a medal." I wasn't lying then.

"Have you given us any honest answers?" the director asked. I just looked at her. Hadn't I fooled her at all?

"We talk to a lot of girls," the director said. "With a lot of street smarts. We have to be even smarter."

I could think of nothing to say in answer to that.

"Okay," she said, standing up. "I hope you believe at least some of what you've told us. As of now, you'll be released a week from Friday. Your final placement is still being considered, but we'll let you know once it's been decided."

I called Shatasia at the group home and this time I got her and she had time to talk.

"Dallas!" she cried. I couldn't remember anybody else ever sounding that glad to hear from me. "How you doin', girl-friend?"

"Okay. My new roomate's a—you know, that word we get in trouble for saying at GRC. How are *you* doing?"

"This place is bad news. Stayin' out of trouble is a joke around here. Nobody's payin' much attention, so we do pretty much anything we want. One of the girls is even dealin' from here. But I go to school and do my work. And I get to see Sharly every day. I love that part."

"You think you're going to be okay?"

"I'm hangin' on by my toenails, girl. The only thing keeps me straight is my baby. But goin' backwards would be real easy. When you gettin' out?"

"Soon. I'm thinking about going to a group home, too. I'm not crazy about going home."

"You better be plenty sure you don't want to go home. One of these places might not be better."

"It will be, take my word for it. I'll be coming to see you as soon as I can."

"All *right*. You can come with me to see Sharly. She's gettin' a new word almost every day."

"Teach her to say Dallas," I said. "And hang on."

"I'm hangin'," she said. "You can call me every day if you want to."

"Okay," I said, and we hung up.

There was a food fight that night at dinner that came out of nowhere. Lupe, the new girl who'd seen Damaris at Juvie, said she missed going salsa dancing, and Roma said she could just imagine how Lupe would look doing that, in a too tight skirt, with her bare belly hanging over the waistband, and Lupe lobbed a spoonful of mashed potatoes that hit Roma in the forehead. Then everybody was throwing food at Roma. We'd been dying to do something like that for a long time.

It was over in minutes, the p.o.'s hurrying into the mess to stop it and everyone ending up with food splattered on them. I was sure that, without the coaches, the food fight would have raced into big-time violence, catching up even those of us who'd been here awhile and were supposed to be getting better at controlling ourselves. I could feel the fascination of it myself, and I had never been someone who was drawn to violence. Threat and surprise were my usual weapons, but I knew violence was effective in a way that nothing else was, and I could feel its allure, the thrill and challenge of being stronger, smarter, meaner than anyone else.

We were all sent to our rooms, and Roma, who had been on the receiving end of most of the thrown food, was allowed to go to the showers to clean up. Her pretty lemon-colored outfit was probably totaled. What a shame.

"I hate that bitch Roma," Lupe muttered to me as we walked down the hall to our rooms. "Thinks she's so much better than anybody, with her matching clothes and her rich girl's hair. She's the same as us. We all have the same mind."

She went into her room and slammed the door. In my room, where I still looked at the other bureau expecting to find pictures of Sharly, I wondered if what Lupe said was true. *Did* we all have the same mind? Was there something wrong with our minds that made us criminal even against our wills? How else to explain someone like Roma who'd had every advantage, and someone like Toozdae who'd had everything go wrong for her, ending up in the same place?

Oh, Dixie Lee, did you poison my blood with a shot of your own outlaw instincts?

Everybody except Roma got twenty-four hours' room confinement for the food fight. The prospect of being shut up in my room for a single day made me consider for the first time what *real* prison would be like. I'd been fooling myself if I thought I'd already experienced it. In comparison, GRC was more like some cut-rate boarding school, with classes and P-E and group and free time every day, in a place where the p.o.'s, like a flock of conscientious sheepdogs, were always watching, always herding us along, nudging us toward the right ways, the ways they wanted us to learn to follow for ourselves.

In a real prison we'd have spent a lot more time locked down in rooms that weren't as nice as these. We probably wouldn't be treated like people who had the potential to be something other than what we were, no matter how much we resisted. The staff's encouragement and goading indicated we were worth salvaging, even when we said we didn't want to be, even when we acted as if we couldn't be, even when we ourselves didn't believe we could be.

Roma came in from the shower. "What a creature that Lupe is," she said, drying her hair with a towel. "She's the kind who'll get in a fight right under a cop's nose, just because she can't control herself. The only way to keep doing what you want to do is to be smart about it. She'll spend her life in places like this."

"What are you talking about?" I said. "You're in here, too. What makes you think you're better than Lupe?"

"Please," she said. "Lupe's a victim of her own blind impulses. I'm someone who thinks things through, who makes plans, who knows what she's doing."

"So what?" I said. "You're still in here. And for the second time."

"Bad luck," she said. "That's the one thing I can't control. Luck." She sat on her bed, brushing her hair in shining sweeps.

She's the same as Lupe, I thought. And so am I. The only difference is, I know it and she doesn't. We all believed luck could keep us from getting caught, that what we were doing wasn't really wrong—that it was even justified because of our need for it. We all *did* have the same mind. How far was that mind from Sylviana's, or Dahlia's? How big a step was it to get there?

169

TWENTY-THREE

Connie brought me a package of discharge papers I had to read.

"Your request for other than home placement has been approved," she said. "I must say I'm surprised."

"Why do you think I got it?" I asked.

"Maybe because your father wanted it, too, and there are no other relatives for you to go to."

"He said that?"

She flipped some pages. "Says here, let's see . . . 'The father indicated that such placement might be beneficial for both Dallas and himself, as they have not, in spite of all his efforts, been able to achieve a method of functioning well together. He doesn't believe he can have any influence on her behavior.' "

" 'A method of functioning well together,' " I repeated. "That's one way of putting it. The truth is, we don't function at all." I didn't even want to think about ". . . in spite of all his efforts . . ." What efforts would those be? Pizzas and videos? Continuing to think I was doomed to become my mother? And that business about influence—making it my fault that we didn't get along. "Where will I go?"

"A group home," she said. "For another nine months. Then you can go home. By that time, you'll be pushing eighteen. You

170

can be making plans for going it on your own, if you want to. But who knows? Maybe you and your father will have figured out a way to get along together."

"And maybe pigs will talk," I said.

"Maybe they will," Connie said.

I called Shatasia to tell her, but she wasn't there and nobody knew where she was. I crossed my fingers for her, that she hadn't gone backwards.

I was going home for my final furlough before my release. I wasn't sure why, except that it was already scheduled and nobody had bothered to cancel it.

I promised myself I wasn't going to say anything to my father about the group-home placement. Why bring it up when it was what we both wanted?

Only it was too near the top of my mind and it came out anyway.

On the way home in the car on a rainy Saturday morning, I blurted, "So you think the group-home thing is a good idea."

"Don't you?" he asked. "You're the one who wanted it."

I looked out the window. "You didn't object."

"Would it have done any good if I had?" He kept his eyes on the road. "It never has before."

I wanted to argue with him, but I couldn't. He was right. I wouldn't have paid any attention if he had objected. It would have been just one more way he was trying to control me. But the perverse part of me, the part that kept me awake at night arguing with itself, wanted him to have resisted, at least a little bit, letting go of me so easily.

"So you give up," I said. The word I left out was *me*. So you give *me* up.

"Are you suggesting I should do otherwise?" He seemed to be talking to me from a great distance, his voice faint and hollow.

What *was* I suggesting? For as long as I could remember, it seemed that all I wanted was for him to quit bugging me— about my manners, about my behavior, about my language. At the same time that I wanted him to quit bugging me, I still wanted him to be completely attentive to me, but only in an adoring, worshipful way. What I got was a sort of gypsy curse— lots of attention, but of the wrong kind.

And now, letting go of even that made me feel the way I did just before I got the flu: shaky and clammy, with a headache getting ready to explode behind my eyes. I pinched the bridge of my nose and looked up. My father cast a quick glance at me and turned back to his driving.

"You okay?" he asked.

"Fine."

"Do you *want* to come home?" he asked, concentrating fiercely on the wet road.

"What do you mean by home?" I asked, deliberately being difficult, marking time while I thought. Did I want to? The home I wanted to go to wasn't the one he lived in. A group home wasn't either, according to Shatasia. But those were the only choices I had. Those were what I'd be saying yes or no to.

He frowned. "Home," he said. "Where I live. Where you lived until you—"

"No," I snapped. If he hadn't started up with that same old stuff, always ready to catalogue my crimes, maybe . . . "No," I said again.

His shoulders went up and then down. Was he disappointed? Relieved? Disgusted?

Instead of putting the car in the garage the way he usually did, he left it at the curb, even though it was raining. Ready for a quick getaway if he couldn't stand being around me for another second? An invitation to me to steal it and disappear? Or maybe just an easy way to get it washed.

This time, it was Chinese food and a video. I was sick of pizza, too, so we'd finally stumbled onto something we agreed on; the only way we'd managed to function together.

The movie was a no-brainer—a guy and his dog having adventures in Alaska. You knew the bad guys would get what they deserved, that the boy and the dog would survive the snowstorm, the fire, the fall through the ice, and all the other bad stuff, and that the boy and the dog would end up with a nice place to live. It was a feel-good movie, no doubt about it, and as I watched it, I got angrier and angrier. Nothing in that movie had anything to do with real life.

I thought my father would never go to bed. For somebody who was as eager to unload me as he was, he seemed reluctant to leave me alone, even if he didn't have anything to say to me.

Finally, after he cleaned up the kitchen, reboxed the video, plumped sofa cushions, checked door locks, watched the news, and wandered around yawning for a while, he told me good night and went to bed.

I sat up, wide awake, my brain whirring. I couldn't live here, and I didn't like the sound of the group home. I didn't have Shatasia's majigney-foofoo, I knew that, and even she was having trouble on the outs. Without Sharly to keep me from going backwards, I could hardly see the point of leaving GRC. But I'd wanted to be released, and I was going to be. I had to go some-where.

An idea jumped into my head.

I could go anywhere I wanted.

So what if I was assigned to a group home? So what if leaving town, leaving the state, even leaving the country was a probation violation? What did I care? Why did I have to go where somebody else told me to? What was there to hold me here?

I could start over somewhere else, a place where I knew nobody, had no reputation, no record. I could change my name, get a job, live alone. Or not. And then see how long it took for me to get in trouble again.

For some reason, I thought of the Roman mosaics Kate had shown us when I'd first come to GRC—all the broken pieces making up a new picture.

It was then I noticed my father had left his car keys, wallet, and change on the table next to the chair he'd sat in to watch the video. He must have left the wallet out when he paid the guy who brought the Chinese food. As for the car keys, he was always leaving them in different places and then frantically looking for them every morning before he left for work.

The wallet was pure carelessness. He'd never deliberately trust me anywhere near his wallet, especially after my first furlough, when I'd taken the quarters and the twenties.

I took all the cash—forty-three dollars—that was in the wallet, and both credit cards. I decided to take the car, too, since it was still raining. I'd leave it at the bus station or someplace where it would be easily found. Like the responsible person my father didn't believe I'd ever be, I'd make sure it was locked and that the keys weren't in it. He had an extra set at home he could use. If he could find them.

I took my still-packed duffel bag from GRC and let myself silently out the front door. I sat in the front seat with the driver's door partly open and the interior light turned off, inhaling rainy-night smells of sodden grass and wet pavement. I don't know why, but those smells made me feel like crying. They made me think of a life I didn't know: innocent summers of late-night conversations on the porch swing and back-yard family barbecues, swims in a neighbor's pool and picnics in the park. Winters of games and popcorn by the fireplace and hot chocolate after school. I wanted that.

But we had neither a fireplace nor a porch swing. Or any of the rest of it.

I slammed the car door, wincing at the noise I hadn't meant to make. There was no way to start the engine quietly, so I just did it fast.

In front of Pam's, I sat watching the rain make patterns on the windshield. I didn't know why I'd come, except that I felt I had to say goodbye to something.

The patter of the raindrops covered the sound my feet made going up Pam's driveway. Her bedroom window was open to the damp night. With my face against the screen, I could see her in the glow from the night-light she'd never given up, because she was afraid of being alone in the dark. Her nightgown was twisted around her legs and she slept on her back.

There she lay, in her bed with the hand-crocheted spread, in the room with the sponge-painted walls and the antique dresser, in the house with the fresh flowers on the dinner table and the coffee beans ground every morning, probably dreaming about the guy who was once my boyfriend. The boy Pam's mother must be having nightmares about, no matter how persuasive Pam might have been about his rehabilitation potential.

The flare of anger at her and Ray came back, stronger than the first time I'd felt it. How could she be sleeping in that fairy-tale bedroom while I was standing in the rain, not knowing where I'd be spending the next night? How could she have two parents and Ray to care about her, while I had nobody? Why did she get to be luckier than me?

I wanted to kill her. And Ray, too.

As soon as I had that thought, I understood that it was an exaggeration. As angry as I was at Pam, and as envious of her, I knew I could never do her harm. As for Ray, what I needed to do was forget him. The good times with him hadn't been worth what I'd had to put up with to get them. And I had to re-member that both Pam and Ray had given me something I'd needed.

I suddenly knew that it was a very big step from me to Dahlia or Sylviana, a bigger step than I could ever take. Violence, as a routine possibility, was not in me.

And neither was the kind of life Dixie Lee had led. As little as I cared about babies, I knew I could never leave one scream-ing alone in an empty house.

It wasn't true that we all had the same mind.

Pam rolled over and I saw that she was holding something in her arms. I pressed my face closer against the screen. It was a stuffed animal. A rabbit. Just like the ones that Shatasia and Sharly had.

I took a step back, standing in the driveway with the rain coming down on my head. I saw that I'd trampled the flowers in the bed beneath the window. They lay crushed into the mud, their necks broken, their petals strewn.

She hadn't had that rabbit six months ago. Had Ray given it to her? He'd never given me anything except an ankle bracelet that was so cheap the clasp wouldn't stay closed. That, and a hard time.

I stepped into the flowers again and peered through the screen. Pam held the bunny in both arms, his head under her chin, his ears bent down on either side of his face. I'd seen Shatasia sleep that way more times than I could count.

I wanted to sleep like that, with a stuffed bunny that somebody who loved me had given me.

I turned away from the window and went to the car. If it had been any farther away, I might not have made it. The feeling I had was as if all the air had been let out of me, as if all my bones had been removed.

My wet clothes soaked into the seat, but I couldn't move. I sat with my forehead on the steering wheel and wept in an uncontrollable torrent. Whoever had told me that tears back up inside you until they finally have to come out was right. There was no way pinching my nose could hold that flood back.

No matter where I went, no matter how tough I was or how rotten, no matter how loud I whistled Kate's great attention-getting whistle, none of it would get me what I wanted. There was no way for me to get that. I would never have a mother, whether it was one with cowboy boots and bad habits or one with a coffee-bean grinder and a subscription to *Good Housekeeping*. I would never have a father who thought the sun, moon, and stars rose over my head. I would have to buy my own stuffed rabbit. Or steal it.

And what good would that do? More stealing, more intimidating, more threatening would bring me—what? Some good times, some kicks, a bunch of stuff I probably didn't even want, and, eventually, some more time locked up, I couldn't doubt that. But I didn't know how to be anyone different.

Oh, the p.o.'s told us: be responsible, be dependable, sacrifice; and the bedtime stories urged us on with poems and fables; and Nolan pestered us about choices. But the struggle to get where they wanted us to go seemed too hard, too impossible.

Only in Shatasia and in some of the books Kate had given me had I been able to see someone actually making that struggle, seen how painful the effort could be. How unending.

If I could just sit in a room somewhere, reading, trying on other people's lives, maybe I could find a place for myself that felt better than where I was, a place that could make me feel full.

I lifted my head. Why *couldn't* I sit in a room and read? Who would care? I had to be in school to satisfy the terms of my probation, so why couldn't I loot the school library and read until my eyes fell out?

I started the car and drove through the empty, wet streets. Past my old elementary school, past stores where I'd stolen clothes, past parks where I'd gotten high, past the golf course with its memories of Ray, past Ray's house, where there was a light on in the kitchen. The rain sputtered and then stopped, and I kept driving.

TWENTY-FOUR

It was after four when I brought the car home. I returned my father's keys to the table where he'd left them, put his money and his credit cards back in his wallet, and went to bed.

When I got up the next day, just before noon, I still felt those flu symptoms I'd felt on the drive home from GRC: light-headed, achy, slow, as if I was just coming down with, or just getting over, a long illness.

"Where were you last night?" my father asked when I shuffled into the kitchen.

I looked at him the way new English speakers do when they think they've understood what you said but they aren't sure.

"You know what I'm talking about," he said. "There are fifty-three miles on the car's odometer that weren't there yesterday."

"Okay, okay. I went for a ride. No big deal."

"Fifty-three miles is no big deal? I guess you didn't get caught."

"At what?"

"At whatever you were doing with my car."

"There's no law against driving around, as far as I know," I said. At least, not as long as he didn't consider it car theft, which

179

he was certainly capable of doing. It was a probation violation, which, of course, he knew.

"You think I should believe you were just driving around? With your history?"

I poured myself some juice. "Believe what you want. You always do." I was too wiped out for this. The irony—a word I'd learned from Kate—of being accused of something I hadn't done, after getting away with so much that I actually *had* done, was not lost on me, but I felt too punk to really enjoy it.

"You know," he said, "you had me going yesterday in the car. Talking about the group home. I thought there might be a chance we could make it work if you came back here. I thought I was hearing that in your voice. But I was way off the mark, wasn't I? Way off."

"If you think so," I said. I drank the juice. "I don't feel very good. I think I'd like to go back to GRC early. I'm only guessing, but I don't think you'll mind taking me, will you?"

"Not if that's what you want."

"I'll go get dressed." I turned to leave the room.

"Dallas," he said.

I stopped but didn't look back at him.

"I'm not going to report this." I heard him sigh. "What's the point? You don't change, no matter what the penalty is. I'm tired of being the ogre."

Good, I was tired of it, too. If he was waiting for my thanks, he didn't get it. I headed for my room.

I slept in the car and again in my room, in spite of Roma rustling around with her magazines and her letter writing. When I didn't want to get up for dinner, Barbara took my temperature and it was a hundred and one. She called the nurse, who gave me some aspirin and hustled me off to the infirmary in case I was contagious. She told me to keep sleeping. No problem.

Monday, I was in bed again all day. Hundred and one, aspirin, tea and toast. In my head, I was somewhere else, floating, drifting, free from everything I knew. It was like a vacation for my mind—getting far away without moving.

Tuesday, ninety-eight point six, but too wobbly to do much.

Wednesday, up, dressed, back on duty. But my mind was having reentry problems, like somebody who's had to come home from vacation too soon. It was rested and tan but not ready to go back to work. I liked the feeling of having a head that was slow and distracted, the feeling that somebody up there was thinking about rearranging the furniture, coming up with a new look, a more relaxed, vacation attitude.

Thursday, the same thing, with more of the sense that mind-furniture was being moved.

"You okay?" Lolly asked me at lunch. "You seem sort of, I don't know, vacant."

"I've been sick," I said. "I'm feeling better but still a little weird."

"Yeah?" she said. "How about some jump rope at P-E?"

Lolly's cure-all. Well, you had to find what worked for you. I thought of what jumping rope might do to my newly arranged mind-furniture and said, "I don't think I'm up to that yet. But it'll make me feel better just to watch you."

"I'll give you a show, girl," she said. And she did.

That evening I called Shatasia to tell her when I was getting out. She invited me to go to church Sunday with her and Sharly and Gram and the little kids. I said okay.

. . .

Friday afternoon, I stood in my room with my packed suitcase, waiting for my ride to the group home. Everybody else was in class. I'd said goodbye at lunch and they'd told me good luck, and stay out of trouble, and then they'd laughed and said we'd probably be seeing each other back here again someday. I couldn't say for sure they were wrong.

I picked up my suitcase in one hand and a paper shopping bag in the other and stood, waiting. The shopping bag held my goodbye gift from Kate—all the books I'd read in the last six months: *The Member of the Wedding, The Road to Oz, To Kill a Mockingbird, Little Women, The Secret Garden, Charlie and the Chocolate Factory, The Martian Chronicles, The Wind in the Willows, Ordinary People, The Little Prince.*

And on top of them all lay the guidebook to Texas that Nolan had given me. I was going traveling and I needed to know the way.